# MURDERED IN MONTEROSSO

# MURDERED IN MONTEROSSO

## TRAVEL P.I., BOOK 3

### ZARA KEANE

BEAVERSTONE PRESS

Published by Beaverstone Press GmbH (LLC)

eBook ISBN: 978-3-03938-020-6
Paperback ISBN: 978-3-03938-019-0
Hardcover ISBN: 978-3-03938-018-3
Large Print Paperback ISBN: 978-3-03938-022-0
Large Print Hardcover ISBN: 978-3-03938-023-7

*M*y estranged brother's text message was about as welcome as an outbreak of crotch crabs. Actually, with the benefit of hindsight, I'd have preferred pubic lice. I didn't like surprises. I especially didn't like surprises involving my crazy family derailing my career plans.

Before my phone heralded impending doom, I was in a buoyant mood. After months of hope and hard work, I, Angel Doyle, semi-reformed thief and accidental P.I., was about to realize my dream. I was in a rental car with my friend Sidney, speeding toward Zürich Airport. We were on our way to Florida and an all-expenses-paid P.I. training camp. In six months, Sidney and I would be fully qualified private investigators and full-time employees of the Omega Group, the supersecret international P.I. agency based in Nice, France, that my mother co-ran with her ex-husband.

Scoring a job with the Omega Group was my dream come true—Sidney's, too. And it was right within our grasp. Or it had been, until thirty seconds ago, when my phone had pinged with news of my brother Del's latest imbroglio.

"Hey, earth to Angel." Sidney took one hand off the steering wheel and waved it in front of my face. "You feeling okay? Was the weapons-grade espresso I bought you too strong, even by your stomach-stripping standards?"

I put my phone facedown on my lap and forced a smile. "The coffee's fine. I'm just tired."

Sidney's expression radiated skepticism. I didn't blame him. Lacking his years at drama school, I sounded as believable as a politician denying a sex scandal. The sick sensation in my stomach turned into a cramp. I couldn't drag Sidney into this mess. He'd be devastated if I told him I was considering skipping our flight. And if I told him why, he'd insist on accompanying me to Italy.

His gaze lingered on me for an uncomfortable moment before he returned his attention to the snow-dusted motorway. "I get it. We've had an insane weekend."

This was the understatement of the millennium. Over the last couple of days, Sidney and I had battled a blizzard, vanquished violent criminals, and rescued a teenager from a literal ticking bomb. Our success in cracking our case had finally convinced my mother we'd make excellent additions to her team. She'd pulled strings to secure two last-minute places in a six-month P.I. boot camp.

A boot camp that I might have to bail on.

My fingers tensed around my phone, but I didn't pick it up. I didn't need to reread Del's message. When his text had arrived, I'd stared at the screen so hard the words had seared into my brain with laser-like precision.

> *Is what Dad says true? Are you some kind of P.I.?*
> *'Cause I need your help. Monterosso al Mare, Italy.*
> *Life or death. Please come, sis. You're the only one I*
> *can trust.*
> *Del xx*

Eight months of no contact, and now this mad missive? What on earth had my brother gotten himself into this time? And how did our father know about my P.I. experience? I hadn't spoken to Dad in almost two years.

Del and I were half-siblings and shared the dubious honor of a career criminal father. Dad was a low-level crook working for a mid-tier London gangster. Two years ago, I'd given evidence against my abusive ex-boyfriend—Dad's boss's son.

Instead of supporting me, my paternal family had branded me a traitor.

Following the fallout, Del had been the only one to keep in touch. I didn't kid myself that he'd chosen my side. More likely, he'd simply forgotten that I was persona non grata. That would be typical of Del. He'd always been slow on the uptake. For months, he'd continued to include me in silly forwards and generic "Yo, whazzup?"–style messages. Nothing personal. Nothing that showed he cared.

Earlier this year, he'd gone radio silent. I was hurt, but not surprised. I assumed he'd finally gotten the memo. Eight months had passed, and my brother hadn't responded to my attempts to get in touch.

Until today.

What's that trite saying? Be careful what you wish for? Yeah. Totally that.

Sidney flipped the indicator and filtered into the lane for the Zürich Airport exit. "We'll have enough time to grab breakfast before our flight. Seeing as we checked in online and just have carry-on baggage, all we need to do is drop off the rental car and get through security."

Our lack of baggage wasn't planned. The Swiss assignment had wrapped up yesterday, leaving us no time to get back to our house in France to pack our stuff. We'd buy clothes once we reached the US. Until then, we each had a small backpack with essentials. The idea of an imminent shopping trip thrilled the fashion-conscious Sidney. All I cared about was weather-appropriate clothing, regardless of my location.

I closed my eyes and tried to rally my racing thoughts. There were several explanations for Del's message. Few reflected well on my brother. None boded well for me.

The most likely scenario was that Del had fallen afoul of a London gang and fled to Italy to hide out. Depending on what sort of scam he'd pulled, it might be the life-or-death situation he described. Or he might simply be on a drug-fueled high.

Memories of past Del disasters flashed before me like a Worst-Of clip collection. The dude was a bona fide mayhem magnet. Take the time he'd forgotten a sports bag full of cash on the London Underground, necessitating a trip to Morocco to outrun his gangster boss. Or the art gallery heist when he'd mistaken an unmarked police vehicle for his getaway car. Del's life was a litany of calamities worthy of an Oscar-winning slapstick comedy. The best part? He had a tendency to drag others into his disaster du jour. Today, it was apparently my turn.

Sidney took the exit, and the airport buildings loomed into view—gray and snow-dipped against the pale blue sky. I had to decide what to do, but my heart beat so fast I could barely breathe, let alone think. I prided myself on my ability to keep my head, but my nerves were shot after yesterday. In the space of twenty-four hours, I'd survived an ambush, two explosions, and a shoot-out. No wonder my fight-or-flight mode was permanently on.

I inhaled slowly and held my breath, allowing my stomach to expand. All I'd wanted was to wish my brother a happy birthday. I'd assumed he'd ignore my text, just as he'd ignored all the others I'd sent him over the last eight months. I hadn't expected my message to generate such a response.

With a controlled exhale, I picked up my phone and began to type. Then I stopped, my thumb hovering over the delete button. Knowing Del, it'd require several incoherent replies for me to decipher the mess he'd landed himself in on this occasion. Calling was the smarter move.

The connection went straight to voicemail. Frustrated, I made a couple more attempts. When I received voicemail for the third time, I released a silent sigh. I loathed leaving voice messages, but it seemed I had no choice. I kept it terse and to the point. "Hey, I got your text. Call me back ASAP."

Aware of Sidney sitting beside me, I tried to keep my voice neutral. I needn't have bothered. My friend had an unerring ability to pick up on other people's emotions, and he was particularly good at reading mine.

He glanced my way, a crease marring his otherwise smooth forehead. "What's wrong?"

"Nothing." Catching his pointedly raised eyebrow, I amended my statement. "Nothing I can't handle."

The crease in his forehead deepened. "That sounds ominous. Who are you trying to call? Your mother? Is there a problem with the boot camp?"

"There's no problem with the course." Or there wouldn't be, if I got on that plane.

I massaged my temples and ran through my options. Could I drive to Italy, find Del, and then fly to Florida before class started? Unlikely. However, I could book a flight from an Italian airport and fly out tomorrow. I'd be a day late, but I'd plead a family emergency. Depending on whatever Del was embroiled in, it wouldn't be a lie.

When Sidney pulled into a space in the rental car company's parking lot, I still hadn't heard from my brother. The concern that had gnawed at me since I'd first read his message had morphed into a full-blown, bile-inducing panic. An icy trickle of sweat slithered down my spine. What should I do? Drop everything and run to Del's rescue? For all I knew, he'd been out of it when he'd composed that text. It had the hallmarks of a bad trip. But what if he was in genuine danger?

Sidney unbuckled his seat belt. "We'd better get moving. A shuttle bus to the terminal leaves in five minutes."

Fear had switched on my stomach's high-speed spin cycle. I reached into the space under the dashboard computer and groped for the key fob. My fingers closed around it with white-knuckled strength, mainly to stop them from shaking. Drug-fueled hoax or not, my brother's message had pushed me close to a panic attack. Why was my reaction this intense? Del and I had been close as kids, but we'd drifted apart by our late teens, long before he'd gone no-contact eight months ago. Old times' sake? A stronger sibling bond than I'd assumed we shared? A premonition of danger?

Still clutching the key, I climbed out of the car.

Sidney leaned into the boot and took out our backpacks, unfurling to his full height. He was so much taller than me—not that beating my five feet two was difficult. His skinny frame made him appear even taller than his six feet two. He had an angular face with enormous blue eyes, a straight nose, and cheekbones sharp enough to cut granite. His were the sort of uniquely striking looks that'd fit right in on a Paris runway.

He shrugged his backpack over his shoulders and handed me mine, examining one of my loose curls. "I know you're not convinced, but I love your natural shade."

"Don't you mean my *unnatural* natural shade?" I quipped. "Dying my hair back to strawberry blond hardly embraces Mother Nature."

In a fit of drunken celebration before we left for Florida, I'd allowed Sidney to dye my hair, changing my curls back to something resembling my natural color for the first time in a decade. His handiwork thrilled him. I felt uncomfortably *seen*. Until I'd woken up this morning and seen my reflection through sober eyes, I hadn't realized how much my dyed hair was part of my self-defense strategy. A reaction I'd ponder later, when I had time to navel-gaze.

He nudged me with my backpack, bringing me back to the here and now. "Why don't you check the car for anything we forgot? I'll drop off the key."

I took my backpack from Sidney's outstretched hand, but I didn't release my grip on the key. For all Del's faults, I couldn't abandon him. Even if it meant temporarily abandoning my course.

"I'm sorry, mate," I blurted. "Something's come up. I'll catch a later flight and join you tomorrow."

This time, both of Sidney's blond eyebrows arched into his shock of fair hair. "Are you serious? What's so important that you need to ditch the flight at the last second?"

I swallowed past a painful lump in my throat. "I'll tell you once I've dealt with it. Promise."

"Not good enough, Angel. You've been angling for this opportunity ever since we moved to Nice. Why would you bail on the chance to train to be a private investigator?" Concern tinged his tone, but his stare was so intense it felt like a mind probe.

I shifted my weight from one leg to the other, dropping my gaze from Sidney's confused face to my scuffed boots. "I'm sorry," I repeated. "I'm bailing on this flight, not on the course. I'll catch a later flight."

"Does your sudden change of mind have anything to do with that text message you got in the car? Who were you trying to call?"

I moved to the driver's side of the rental car without meeting his eye. "I'll tell you all about it when I get to Florida. The cocktails are on me."

"You can't just leave with no explanation, Angel. And what about the rental contract? The car's due back now."

"I'll call them later. Don't worry. I'll cover the extra cost."

His sigh expressed exasperation. "The cost isn't my concern. You're stressed, and I want to know why. No way you'd willingly turn your back on the opportunity to take this P.I. boot camp."

"I'm not quitting the course. I'm just not catching this flight." If I looked at him, I'd burst into tears.

I'd only known Sidney since July, but the situations we'd been through since our first encounter had made us close. Well, as close as I allowed myself to get to anyone. Regardless, he was a friend. A good friend. Probably the best friend I'd ever had.

Which was why I couldn't tell him the truth. Sidney would never let me go to Italy on my own. He'd insist on tagging along to help, even though he wanted to be a professional P.I. just as badly as I did. My showing up a day late for our boot camp was a major no-no. For all I knew, I'd get the proverbial middle finger and find myself on the next flight back to France. I couldn't let Sidney share that risk.

On impulse, I closed the space between us and hugged him tight. He smelled of shampoo, posh scent, and dependability. My tight shoulders relaxed, and a comforting warmth replaced the icy tension.

And then the text message flashed through my mind in glowing neon letters—a garish reminder of what I had to do.

I broke the embrace and stepped back, my cheeks growing warm. I didn't do physical affection. My sudden desire to hug Sidney had to be caused by stress.

Sidney stared down at me, agog and slightly pink. He affected a laugh. "Angel Doyle engaging in a PDA? The Apocalypse must be nigh."

"Not quite." I shifted my weight from one leg to the other. "I'll call you when you land in Florida and let you know when I'll arrive. It'll be tomorrow at the latest."

Without waiting for a response, I leaped into the car and started the engine, neatly reversing out of our space and speeding toward the exit. In the rearview mirror, Sidney watched me go for a second, hands in his hair, mouth open. Then his lips formed words I couldn't hear. He ran after the car, waving for me to stop.

Doubt crept over me. Did I want to face the Del situation on my own? No. How likely were Sidney and

I to miss the start of our course if I booked us seats on a flight out of Italy this evening? Depending on the connections, we could still make it.

I switched my foot to the brake, about to press down on the pedal when my phone pinged with an incoming text. My innards lurched, and my clammy palms grew clammier. Ignoring road safety regulations, I pulled my phone out of my pocket and scanned the screen.

*Can't talk right now. Not alone. Can't give deets. I think my phone's hacked. Remember our hideout when we were kids? Meet me at the place that looks like it. Four p.m., Italian time. Come alone. No cops.*

Our hideout? But that was in London. What place in Monterosso, a town I'd never been to, resembled the abandoned shed we'd transformed into our childhood fort? A shaft of unease pierced the dented armor of my self-control. The first message might have resulted from a bad trip, but the second? No. Del was in trouble.

I tossed the phone onto the passenger seat and took a last look in the rearview mirror. Sidney was still running after me, a lanky blond blob growing smaller by the second. If Del was in genuine danger, no way was I involving my friend. Blinking back tears, I hit the gas.

## 2

It was three-thirty when I spotted the first signpost for Monterosso al Mare. The navigation system's prediction of a six-and-a-half-hour drive had become a lie two hours ago, and my anxiety was at an all-time high. Heavy snowfall in Switzerland had slowed me down. Although the weather had improved markedly once I'd neared the Swiss-Italian border, the likelihood of making it to the mysterious meeting point by four was dwindling with each sharp twist of the mountain road.

My gaze flitted to the cloud-dappled baby-blue sky. Sidney was on a plane, heading to sunny Florida—a plane I should've been on. I didn't regret ditching him at the airport. That decision fell into the being mean to be kind category. Putting my place in the P.I. boot camp in jeopardy was one thing. Wrecking Sidney's chance to attend was out of the question.

Plus, there was the prickly matter of my mother. My French *maman* and I didn't have the easiest relationship. It had taken persuasion, hard work, and a dash of ingenuity to persuade her to give Sidney and me a shot as private investigators. When she found out I'd skipped my flight, she'd be livid. I had to make it to Florida before she discovered I'd gone AWOL. Otherwise, she'd rescind the offer of a job at the Omega Group, chuck me out of her villa, and send me packing back to London.

So, no, I didn't regret abandoning Sidney, but that didn't stop me from wishing he were here now. Between us, we had a knack for slotting puzzle pieces of information into the right places. We'd found ourselves in a series of hairy situations during the four months of our friendship, and we'd always gotten out of them together.

This time, I was on my own.

The mountain road narrowed into a blade-sharp curve, forcing me to hit the brakes. For the next few minutes, I shelved all thoughts of the Del situation and concentrated on avoiding an accident. After a steep climb, I caught my first glimpse of the sea, glistening a glorious blue green in the sunlight. From this point on, the road meandered down to sea level and the tiny streets of Monterosso.

Between bouts of worrying about my brother, I'd used the drive to Italy to extend the lease on the rental car and research my destination. Thanks to my phone's trusty voice assistant, I'd gleaned the essentials, even if no app could figure out where in the town resembled our childhood hideout. Monterosso was the most populous of the five coastal villages that formed Cinque Terre, a picturesque national park on the Italian Riviera. The park was popular with hikers, who used the old mule trails along the cliffs to walk from town to town. A robust train service connected the five towns, and a frequent ferry operated during the summer months. Car traffic was restricted, and many areas were pedestrian-only.

Seeing as it was November and low tourist season, I had no trouble finding a space in the public parking lot on the seafront. I climbed out of the car and inhaled the welcome salty tang of the sea. Although the weather was warmer than in Switzerland, few people braved the Mediterranean Sea in November. The only swimmers on the beach today were a hardy pair of body surfers and a playful Labrador paddling in the surf.

Even after months of living in Nice, I hadn't lost my love of the Med. Now I was seeing it from a different angle—from the Italian coast as opposed to the French. While the Med had the same distinctive colors, the rest of the scenery differed from Nice. Monterosso was comprised of groups of brightly colored buildings dotting the hillside and rolling down to the shore. Further along the craggy coastline, a cluster of colorful facades clung to the cliff. This must be Vernazza, the second of the five towns. Cinque Terre was famed for its dramatic coastline, complete with steep cliffs and invisible inlets. No wonder the area had once been as popular with pirates as it was with smugglers today.

I narrowed my focus to my immediate surroundings. The parking lot was in Fegina, a village amalgamated into Monterosso that was now referred to as the new town. A pedestrian tunnel linked the new town with the old—I could just make out the start of the tunnel at the end of the seafront. On either side of the car park, the beach stretched until it reached jagged outcroppings of rock. The street parallel to the beach boasted a plethora of brightly painted shops, cafés, restaurants, and the town's train station.

Sweat beaded on the back of my neck, and a prickly feeling crept over my shoulders. I'd experienced this sensation before. Someone was watching me.

My heartbeat kicked up a notch. My chest tight, I spun around, my gaze darting from side to side. There weren't many people about. A few kids and their parents hung out at a small beachside playground. An elderly couple walked an equally elderly dachshund down the beach. One or two delivery bikes whizzed by. No one paid me the slightest attention.

I had to get a grip and can the paranoia. Whatever mess Del was in, no one knew who I was. All the same, I couldn't shake the persistent prickle of unease. What if Del was in genuine danger? And if so, was I walking into a trap unarmed? Sidney and I had planned to take only carry-on with us on the flight to Florida, so I had no weapons with me, not even my trusty Swiss Army knife. Regardless, I had to act fast. I had ten minutes left to interpret Del's cryptic message and locate a place that looked like our childhood hideout. And I hadn't a clue where to start.

I took a deep breath of salty air and willed my racing thoughts into a game plan. My best bet was to stop at the shops and cafés facing the beach. I had no idea why my brother was in Monterosso or how long he'd been here. But if Del had stayed for any length of time, the locals would remember him. He was that kind of guy. They'd have chatted with him, gotten drunk with him, or banned him from their premises.

Before embarking on my quest to track down my idiot brother, I swapped the fugly orange winter coat I'd worn on my Swiss assignment for a lighter jacket. Then I dumped the contents of my backpack into the boot, grabbing a protein bar, a water bottle, and my purse. The energy bar—cookies and cream flavor—was a gag gift from my other roommate, Luc. He was an experienced private investigator for the Omega Group, the alpha male to Sidney's beta, and my secret crush. Horrified by my taste in sweet treats, Luc had presented me with a selection pack of protein bars based on popular chocolate bar flavors. He'd expected me to react with revulsion. Instead, I'd promptly eaten one and packed the rest for my flight.

I shoved my loot into my jacket pockets and locked the car. It was time to find Del, sort out whatever mess he'd gotten himself into, and book the next available flight to Florida.

Across the street, my determination faltered when I registered all the Closed signs. I'd blanked the fact that many businesses took an extended afternoon break. Most places would be open again by five, but I couldn't wait that long. I needed insta-info about my brother and tumbledown sheds.

The door to a yellow-painted shopfront swung open, and a glorious wave of freshly ground coffee wafted out. The looping cursive letters over the door read Gelateria Arturo. I wasn't in the mood for ice cream or coffee, but at least this joint appeared to be open.

I nodded at the dark-haired woman and toddler exiting the gelateria, the child clutching a small cone. The mother held the door for me. "*Grazie*," I said and stepped inside.

The ice cream parlor was like being whisked back to the 1950s. Vintage posters of Italian advertisements decorated the walls, and an old-fashioned soda fountain dominated the counter that ran along the side of the room. At the back, an enormous coffee machine glugged and hissed behind a display of every conceivable ice-cream flavor. Two old guys sat at a table near the ice cream display, a chessboard between them, brows furrowed in concentration. One man wore an apron with Arturo embroidered over the left breast pocket. This must be the proprietor of the establishment. His opponent was a nondescript guy in his seventies whose drab gray clothes matched his drab gray hair.

Neither man looked up when I came in, so I concentrated on the only other person in the room—a perky blonde with jangly loop earrings and a cleavage-baring uniform. I guessed the outfit was intended to match the '50s theme, but the tight bodice and thigh-skimming swing skirt made it look more like a sex shop costume.

The blonde glanced up from the table she was clearing and peered at me through eyelashes so thick it looked like twin centipedes had adhered to her eyelids. "*Buongiorno.*"

I was still on the fence about the best attack strategy, so I winged it. Thankfully, Italian was a language I spoke with reasonable fluency. I launched into a jumbled explanation about an appointment with my brother at a falling-down shed, location unknown.

The blonde blinked her furry lashes and curved her bubblegum-pink lips into a smile. "You can speak English," she said with a pronounced Australian accent. "Major whew. My Italian still sucks donkey balls."

Despite my elevated stress levels, I cracked a laugh.

"I take it you weren't hired for your linguistic skills, then?"

She grinned, transforming her heart-shaped face from plain to pretty. "Arturo hired me for my boobs." She turned to her boss. "Isn't that right, Arturo?"

Keeping his eyes on the game, Arturo emitted a grunt that could've meant anything from outraged denial to hearty assent.

The woman rolled her eyes and carried her tray behind the ice cream display. "I'm Barbie, by the way," she threw over her shoulder. "I only understood bits of what you said in Italian. Something about your brother?"

"Yeah. I'm supposed to meet him." I checked my watch. "Right about now, actually. Problem is, I don't know where."

Barbie pursed her bubblegum lips. "That's a conundrum. Any clues?"

"Can you think of a tumbledown cottage or shed near here? Bonus points if it has a resident rat."

She snorted a laugh. "Are you sure you're not looking for my ex's place? Seriously, though, the hills are littered with abandoned settlements. Take any of the hiking trails, and you'll encounter several. They're practically a tourist attraction."

I bit back a groan. Trust Del to pick a meeting point I'd struggle to find. I sifted through my memories. Was there anything about our hideout that made it stand out? The whole point of the place was that no one went there.

As my mind worked overtime, my gaze fixed on the gleaming red coffee machine. Above it hung a crumpled rogues' gallery of Do Not Serve ex-patrons, ranging from a dog-eared photo of a dude named Pietro taken circa 1960 to a laser-printed snapshot of a very familiar face.

My heart performed a thump and roll. Trademark cocky grin, mop of strawberry-blond curls, and faded T-shirt with the logo of his long-defunct teenage band. What on earth had my brother done to get banned from a gelateria? And why was his unofficial mugshot labeled with the name Jimmy?

## 3

*M*y eyes bugged so hard I thought they'd burst out of my sockets. I jabbed a finger at the photos. "The bloke in the last picture. The one called Jimmy. Do you know him?"

Barbie regarded my brother's photograph with bored disinterest. "Oh, yeah. Everyone knows Jimmy— he's barred from every bar in Monterosso. He's a bit of a lad, if you know what I mean."

Yeah, I knew exactly what she meant. My brother Del—or Jimmy, as he was apparently calling himself in Italy—had an unerring knack for getting into fights and riling the wrong people. And if he'd had time to get banned from every establishment that served booze, he'd been in Monterosso for a while.

"Do you know where Jimmy hangs out these days?" I aimed for nonchalance, but, once again, my lack of acting talent produced the opposite effect on my audience.

Barbie's furry eyelashes flattened. She treated me to a suspicious scrutiny before examining the photographs on the wall. "You're as red-haired and freckled as that drongo. Don't tell me *Jimmy's* your brother?"

Should I admit to being related to a guy she clearly held in low regard? But what was the point of lying about our relationship? I didn't have to reveal Del's real name.

Mind made up, I shot her a rueful smile. "Guilty as charged. I'm supposed to meet him, and the daft sod sent me a rough description of where, but no address." I rolled my eyes. "Totally in character."

And totally true, even if I'd left out the reason for Del's message.

Barbie shook her head. "Jimmy's a character. I can give you his address. It's the same as mine. But he's pulling your leg about the hovel part. We live at the Villa Margherita."

She said the name like it meant something. Which it presumably did, just not to me. "Wait, back up a sec. You live with D—" I performed a rapid course correction. "With my brother?"

"Not in the same apartment." Barbie's tone held just the right amount of aghast. "He and Dani live downstairs. I think her uncle owns the property?"

Who in the wide world was Dani? Del's latest

girlfriend? "That makes sense," I replied, improvising fast. "I can't see that pair affording anywhere fancy."

"Theirs is the smallest apartment at the villa," Barbie conceded, "but it's still a gem of a place. Dani says they're allowed to live there until she goes back to work and they can afford a place of their own again."

This tale stank worse than rotting fish. Why was Dani out of work? How was Del earning his crust? And were my brother and his current squeeze squatters? It wouldn't be the first time Del had made himself at home without an invitation, and it could explain his current predicament. But would a homeowner, however irate, threaten to kill the people occupying his property? Seemed a tad extreme.

My skepticism must have shown on my face. "Are they hoping to stay at the villa permanently?" Barbie asked, misinterpreting my train of thought. "Maybe they can negotiate an affordable rent agreement with Dani's uncle."

"I'm not sure what their long-term living plans are. Do you know them well?"

Barbie considered before answering. "I know Dani better than Jimmy, but we're not close. I've taken her to the hospital a few times because they don't have a car. Jimmy can hardly drive her all the way to Levanto on his Vespa."

"Hardly," I murmured, not having a clue what she was talking about, nor why the unknown Dani needed to go to the hospital. Rehab?

"And I see them at our weekly potluck dinners," Barbie continued. "If you're visiting them at the villa, they're sure to drag you along this evening. Speaking of the villa..." She drew an order pad out of her skirt pocket, scribbled on it in an expansive cursive, and tore the sheet free. "Here's the address. You can wow Jimmy with your detective skills."

I reeled back, momentarily baffled. "How do you know about my detective skills?"

"You solved the puzzle and figured out his address." Barbie winked at me. "No need to mention I helped."

My heart rate settled back to normal. My paranoia was out of control. Barbie couldn't possibly know the contents of my brother's message. And she definitely didn't know he was in danger. "Oh, yeah. That. Thanks for the address." I took the piece of paper and pivoted to leave.

"Hey, wait a sec," Barbie called. "You never told me your name."

Good point. What was my name? The panic crept over me again. What was I supposed to say? I didn't even know Del's fake surname. "Kimmy," I blurted, kicking myself before I'd uttered the final syllable.

Barbie's furry lashes slow-blinked. "Jimmy and Kimmy? Are you two twins?"

I'd already told one lie, and I was too tired to come up with a better alias. "What can I say? Our parents liked rhyming names."

She pondered this a moment, then nodded. "I thought Barbie was a bad name. Parents, eh?"

"Indeed." I forced a smile. "See you around, Barbie."

She grinned. "If I know Jimmy and Dani, I'll see you again in a couple of hours. We love our weekly potlucks."

Back on the street, I checked the address she'd given me. It was four-fifteen, and I was no wiser about where Del wanted us to meet. Was Barbie's hunch correct? Was Del's message his attempt at being clever? Had my brother meant I should meet him at a place the polar opposite of our childhood hideout? I pulled out my phone and reread Del's most recent message. Enlightenment failed to materialize.

I hit the call button.

A wave of relief washed over me when it didn't instantly connect to voice mail, but when there was no answer, my optimism dimmed. I was on the verge of hanging up when a gruff "Who is this?" came through the speaker.

My internal danger alarms switched to red alert. This man had spoken Italian and sounded a couple of decades older than my brother. Where was Del? And who had his phone?

"Who are you?" I demanded in Italian, my voice wobbling along with the rest of me. "I want to talk to Jimmy."

"You must be the sister." The man switched to

excellent English with a touch of the East End of London and the barest trace of an Italian accent. I could practically hear the sneer on his face. "Go home, little girl. Or your brother's as good as dead. And if you call the cops, you and the girl are dead, too."

Before I could deliver a bruising retort, the man disconnected. Stunned, I stared at the screen, breathing hard. What now? If the stranger had Del's phone, he must have Del. That meant wherever Del had intended to meet me was no longer safe.

I stared ahead, unseeing. When my eyes finally focused, they fixed on the sign above the police station, just a few doors down from Arturo's ice cream parlor. Should I ignore the man's warnings and go to the cops?

A prickling awareness trickled down my spine. Someone was watching me. And this time, I wasn't being paranoid.

I reached into my pocket, searching for my trusty pepper spray or my Swiss Army knife. And came up empty. I had no self-defense tools due to air travel regulations. My heart thumped sluggishly against my ribs.

In one fluid movement, I swung around to confront the person tailing me. But there was no one there. The closest people to me were a couple of kids cruising down the pavement on skateboards. They didn't spare me a glance when they zoomed past. An old man smoking a pipe sat on a bench opposite, facing the sea.

Unless he had eyes in the back of his head, he wasn't spying on me.

I breathed in deeply. This skittishness had to stop. It wasn't like me to freak out about every little thing. If I wanted to track down my brother, I had to keep my cool.

I squared my shoulders and cast a long look at the police station. I had a rocky history with law enforcement and a deep distrust of cops. Which made my decision to become a P.I. even more ironic. Or perhaps it explained it. That was a question to ponder when I didn't have a missing brother to locate.

Seeing as the mysterious meeting point was a no-go, I'd head to the villa and speak to Del's girlfriend, Dani. Maybe she could shed light on whatever jam he was in. And she deserved to know some rando was making threats against her.

With steadier fingers than I'd had since Del's text had hit my phone this morning, I plugged the villa's address into my phone's map app. Like many Italian addresses, Villa Margherita had a street name listed, but no house number. Once the app guided me to Via Garibaldi, I'd have to figure out the rest of the way on my own.

As it happened, I didn't have a problem finding Del's Italian residence. The walk to the villa took less than twenty minutes—Monterosso was a small town. I followed my phone's directions away from the touristy seafront and up a steep road into a leafy residential area. And by steep, I mean the sort of slope where if you trip, you don't have far to fall before you face-plant.

The higher I climbed, the larger the houses, and the more land each house occupied. When the residences boasted swimming pools and fancy mosaic name signs, I figured I had to be close. Villa Barbara, Villa Orizzonte, Villa Gia...how many villas could one small town have? I was out of breath and contemplating shedding my jacket when I spotted Del's place.

Villa Margherita was concealed behind a pair of enormous wooden gates framed by high stone walls and lush foliage. I could just make out the gently sloping terracotta roof. An intercom with six doorbells was positioned underneath the mosaic name sign, presenting me with a dilemma. Some nameplates listed the occupants' family name. Others had only an apartment number. Barbie hadn't mentioned the surname Del was using in Italy, and I hadn't thought to ask.

K. Heaton and B. Drake occupied one apartment—presumably Barbie and her flatmate. At least I could eliminate one of the six as a possibility. I similarly discarded S. and R. Ventimiglia and M. Bianchi as nonstarters. That left me with the three apartments labeled only by number—one, five, and six respectively.

Barbie had said Del and Dani lived in the smallest

of the villa's apartments. Would that make theirs one or six? My fingertip moved back and forth before I jabbed on one. For a full minute, nothing happened. I was dithering between pressing a second time or trying the bell for apartment six when the intercom crackled into life.

"If you're Tommaso, I'm not home. If you're a debt collector, I'm dead. But if you're delivering pizza, I'll roll out the red carpet." The voice was male, posh, and decidedly British.

"I'm not Tommaso," I said in English. "Or a debt collector. Or, regrettably, a pizza delivery."

"Then why are you cluttering up my airwaves?" the man snapped waspishly. "No, the villa is not open for tours. No, it won't be open for tours tomorrow or any day this side of the apocalypse. What is wrong with people? Why can't you all leave me alone?"

"I'm happy to leave you alone. I'm here to visit Jimmy and Dani and hit your doorbell by mistake. Can you please buzz me in?"

"Buzz you in? A perfect stranger? What if you're here to steal my hydrangeas?" His outrage rose with each word.

This man was deranged. "I'm not here to steal your hydrangeas. Do hydrangeas even bloom in November? Look, all I want is for you to let me in or let me know which doorbell is Jimmy's."

"Stay right where you are," the voice barked. "I'm coming down."

I wasn't convinced I wanted this rude dude coming anywhere near me. On the other hand, he might open the gate and then I could make a run for it and find Dani's place. I looked around for a potential weapon, but no conveniently placed stout stick presented itself.

A moment later, rusty bolts were drawn back, and the gates opened a fraction. A thin bearded face peered through the crack, blinking at me from behind a pair of orange-tinted spectacles. He darted a glance up and down the street, then opened the gates. "Hurry. We don't want anyone slipping in unnoticed."

The man had to be completely barmy. All the same, this was my chance to get inside the villa's grounds. I hopped across the threshold and found myself in a gravel courtyard complete with a fountain and a discreet entrance to an underground garage.

He slammed the gates shut, bolted them securely, and turned to face me. Seeing him in his entirety did nothing to assuage my impression that my new acquaintance was off his rocker. He wore battered leather sandals and a dirty silk kimono that looked as though it had survived a nuclear war. His few remaining tufts of graying dark hair clung greasily to his scalp, and his bushy, silver-flecked beard and sideburns grew in the unkempt style last favored by 80s conspiracy theorists.

While I'd given him the once-over, he'd treated me to the same. Judging by the twitch of his nostrils, I'd failed his inspection as surely as he'd failed mine.

"Jocelyn Dingus-Cockett," he snapped. "And you are?"

"Jimmy's sister, Kimmy."

The fake name had been borne out of desperation, but I was getting curiously attached to it, particularly its effect on others.

Jocelyn's steel wool eyebrows shot into his receding hairline. "Jimmy and Kimmy?" He infused each syllable with just the right amount of contempt.

"Jocelyn Dingus-Cockett?" I shot back. "In the contest for worst names, I'd say we're about even."

I expected him to take exception, but he merely shrugged. "You may have a point."

I turned and looked up at the villa. It was bigger than I'd expected for a building divided into six apartments and three floors tall. "Can you tell me which is Jimmy and Dani's door?"

"Not so fast." He peered at me over the rims of his ridiculous orange glasses. "How do I know you're who you say you are? I need to ask Dani to identify you before I tell you where she lives."

I met Jocelyn's skeptical gaze head-on. "Good luck with that. Dani and I have never met. I haven't seen my brother in two years."

"A general family falling out? Or a tiff between siblings?"

I shrugged. "Let's just say we're not close."

"And yet here you are." Jocelyn raised his shoulders in an exaggerated shrug. "Funny time of the year to visit Monterosso. Most people want to come in the spring or summer. During the lemon festival in May, the town is packed."

"Depending on how Jimmy and I get along during this visit, maybe I'll come back for some lemonade."

Jocelyn regarded me for a long moment. Finally, he extended a bony finger toward the red door at the bottom left of the building. "That's Dani and Jimmy's place. I'll wait here until you go in. I don't want you making off with my hydrangeas."

The only flowers in evidence were part of an arrangement of cacti. "Dude, I wouldn't know a hydrangea from a geranium, yet I feel confident in saying neither is in bloom."

Jocelyn stood his ground, a belligerent expression creeping over his thin features. "All the same. I don't want you stealing them."

"Potty," I muttered under my breath as I closed the distance between me and the red door. "Absolute nutter."

I knocked on Dani's door. At first, there was no response. Then a cacophony of barking shook the door and rattled the windows. A scramble of paws clattered across a hardwood floor. I staggered back just as an enormous St. Bernard erupted into the courtyard, reared up on its hind legs, and knocked me flat.

# 4

The impact winded me and sent a searing pain through my head. A huge, furry face loomed over me, tongue lolling, before subjecting me to an enthusiastic licking that soaked me from chin to forehead. I struggled to break free, but fifty kilos of dog pinned me in place.

"Bernice," a woman yelled in English. "Bad dog. Get off her right now."

Bernice ignored the newcomer. She continued licking me, with a tongue rough enough to replace my twice-weekly exfoliation routine. And as for her breath...I fought the urge to gag.

The woman repeated the order in shrill Italian. Bernice didn't give a rat's what language was used to yell at her. She'd found a new toy—me—and she wasn't about to give me up.

Thanks to the dog standing on my chest, I couldn't

do more than wheeze. All I could see from this vantage point was fur and a snatch of gravel courtyard. Red-toenailed feet moved into my limited line of vision. This had to be Dani.

"Wipe that smirk off your face, Jocelyn," she snapped in English. "You could have at least helped."

"May I remind you the villa has a no-pets policy, Dani." Jocelyn's voice rose to a hectoring falsetto. "By moving in that monstrosity, you and your boyfriend have violated the sanctity of our home."

"What no-pets policy?" Dani scoffed. "You have five cats. Five. Cats."

"Six cats. Six well-behaved cats. And they don't count as pets. They're my people."

Dani muttered a series of insults in Italian, one of which sounded suspiciously like a slur against Jocelyn's man parts. A moment later, a red ball whizzed past my head. The dog gave a happy yelp, leaped off my chest, and tore off in pursuit of a new treasure.

Before I'd had time to refill my squashed lungs, hands reached down and hauled me to my feet. I found myself face to face with a dark-haired woman of about my age and height—mid-twenties, five feet two or three. She had an adorable snub nose, dimples, and a belly large enough to accommodate quadruplets.

The full import of that belly hit me like a blow to the solar plexus. For the second time since I'd arrived at the Villa Margherita, I took an involuntary step back—and trod on Jocelyn's sandaled feet. He gave an agonized howl that Bernice wasted no time in emulating.

Transfixed by Dani's baby bump, I ignored the cacophony. "You're *pregnant*?"

My tone conveyed horrified disbelief—not the socially correct response when encountering a mother-to-be. But this wasn't just any pregnant woman. If Dani was Del's girlfriend, chances were my idiot brother was the father. I wouldn't trust my brother to look after a goldfish, never mind a baby.

The concern in Dani's eyes vanished, replaced with hostile wariness. "Why do you care if I'm expecting?"

"Because she's the aunt," Jocelyn supplied, smirking at me over Dani's shoulder. "Dani, meet Kimmy, Jimmy's twin sister."

Dani's dark eyes grew flying saucer wide. Her lips parted, then clamped together to form a hard line. From her expression, it was hard to tell if she'd ever heard of Del's sister, or even if she knew his real name. I had no idea how long the two had been a couple. Long enough to make this baby?

"Didn't Jimmy tell you I was coming to visit?" My smile was saccharine sweet. "How remiss of him."

"Jimmy's vague about a lot of things," Jocelyn supplied with a hint of malice. "Starting with when he's going to pay me back for the destruction of my flower beds. I supplied him with an itemized invoice two months ago."

"We don't know what happened to the flowers," Dani said through gritted teeth. "You accused Bernice of digging them up, but Barbie says she saw you down in the garden with a trowel at night. How do we know you didn't wreck your own hydrangeas while under the influence of your herbal tea?"

"Tending to my flowers at midnight is part of my routine. Why would I dig them up? No, that beast of yours was responsible. I guarantee it."

Dani placed her hands on her enormous baby bump and gave a loud whistle. "Bernice, Jocelyn wants to play chase. Go get him, girl."

Bernice dropped her ball, released a series of joyous barks, and made a beeline for Jocelyn.

He emitted a squawk reminiscent of a strangled chicken and fled through the courtyard with the speed of a hunted gazelle.

Dani grabbed my elbow. "Quick. Let's go inside before Jocelyn comes back."

She ushered me through the red door into a charming apartment with an open-plan living space spread out over two half levels. The decor was a seamless combo of vintage and modern. Red, charcoal, and white were the dominant colors. The hallway led directly into the kitchen—all silver chrome and red tiles. A glass-topped table was strewn with papers. Most were black-and-white photocopies of newspaper articles. I strained to get a better look, but Dani had other ideas.

"We need to talk." She half-guided, half-shoved me toward the flight of four steps that led up to the living room. A closed door to my left blocked my view of the rest of the place, but a glass door to my right opened onto a small loggia—a covered balcony with a dining table, lounge chairs, and an area to hang washing. I'd no sooner stepped outside to check it out when Bernice leaped over the stone wall that separated the loggia from the courtyard and skidded to a halt at my feet. She held the red ball between her jaws and gave a plaintive whine.

"Leave our visitor alone," Dani said, carrying a large bone. She gave the bone to the dog and gestured for me to go back inside. "No prying ears in here," she murmured. "Joceyln eavesdrops."

"He's quite the character," I said dryly. "Does he live here full-time?"

Dani scrunched up her nose. "Alas, yes."

"What does Jocelyn do when he's not eavesdropping?"

"He's some sort of writer, but he seems to spend most of his time drinking vile herbal teas and contemplating conspiracy theories."

I laughed. "That fits with my first impression of him."

Dani closed the door to the loggia and dropped into an overstuffed armchair. I took the chair opposite, wincing when my backside made contact with a prickly dog toy. I removed the offending item and settled in the chair.

My host fixed me with a look of steel. "So, *Kimmy*, what brings you to Monterosso?"

"My brother contacted me." I avoided referring to Del by name—either name.

Her steely-eyed look turned molten. "Who sent you? Tomasso?"

"The only Tomasso I know sells pizzas on the beach near my house in France. And, no, he didn't send me anywhere." I changed tack, determined to gain control over the conversation. "Where did you meet my brother?"

Her lips curled into a mocking smile. "Don't you know? Aren't you and your twin brother close?"

"I don't have a twin brother and my name's not Kimmy. I do have a half brother. Three, in fact. But right at this moment, I'm only concerned with the one living here."

Dani's wary expression wavered. "How do I know you're telling the truth?"

I pulled out my purse and found my French national ID card. I handed it to her. "That's me, Angel Doyle. Unlike my half brothers, I'm a dual national. My mother is from Marseilles—not that she'd ever admit it—and my father is Irish but lives in London."

Dani examined my ID, but I could see I'd convinced her. "Okay. Then you know Jimmy isn't my boyfriend's real name."

"I do. But it's time for *you* to cough up some info. Why don't you start by telling me what he's really called?"

"Del, short for Derek." She delivered the words with a sigh.

"Bingo." I sat back and gave her a careful once-over. "You speak excellent English."

"I ought to. My parents spent a small fortune sending me to an English boarding school for a while. I returned to London a couple of years ago."

"And met Del?"

She hesitated, and I detected a flash of fear in her eyes before her shutters slammed into place. "Yes, but it's not as straightforward as you might think."

I cracked a laugh. "Nothing about Del is ever straightforward."

A scratching at the door behind me snagged my attention away from Dani. A plaintive whine followed the scratching. Without waiting for permission, I stood and let Bernice into the living room. The dog pounced on the toy I'd discarded from my chair and settled down for a satisfying chew. Now that I had the leisure to examine the dog, I noted her size.

"Good grief. Is that thing still a puppy?"

Dani nodded. "She's eight months old. She'll be fully grown in a year or two."

"How will she fit in this apartment?"

"She won't. I gave my boyfriend an ultimatum. He needs to rehome her before the baby arrives."

I eyed her baby bump. "Which is when?"

"I'm due in five days."

"And the dog's still here?"

Her lips twisted into a mockery of a smile. "As you can see. But you didn't look me up to discuss Bernice."

"No, I didn't." I drummed the armrests of my chair. "Before you dragged me into the apartment, you said we needed to talk. Do you know where Del is? And do you know why I'm here?"

Dani shook her head, loosening a strand of silky dark hair from her ponytail. Her expression turned from wary to worried. "He didn't come home last night. And he's not answering his phone. When I woke up and saw he wasn't here, I was annoyed, but not worried. He was out last night, celebrating a friend's birthday. I figured he'd had too much to drink and crashed at Marco's place. But it's almost five in the evening, and no word."

"Have you tried calling his friends?"

She inclined her head. "Of course. No one knows where he is. Marco says Del stayed over last night but left before six-thirty. It's only a half hour's walk from Marco's place to the villa. So where is he?"

I performed a rapid calculation. "That means Del contacted me around forty-five minutes after he left his friend's place." I pulled my phone out of my pocket, brought up Del's messages, and handed the device to Dani. "I came to Italy because Del sent me panicked text messages."

41

Dani screwed up her forehead and scanned my screen. Her lips formed silent words.

"Well?" I demanded. "Do these messages mean anything to you?"

She looked up, blinked back tears, and scowled at me. "Why aren't you out looking for him? Did you even go to the meeting point?"

"When I called Del for less vague directions, a stranger answered his phone. A stranger who threatened to hurt Del, you, and me if I went to the police."

The blood drained from Dani's face. She swayed in her chair, and for a moment, I wondered if she'd faint. Then she took a shuddery breath and appeared to pull herself together. "Luigi. Luigi's found us."

"Who's Luigi? What does he want with Del?"

Dani stared at an invisible point above my shoulder, fear etched across her green-tinged face. "Luigi Genero. My husband."

# 5

*I*ce-cold dread seeped into my bones. My brother Del had screwed up plenty of times, but this mess was sprouting poisonous tentacles by the second. "Let me get this straight: Luigi Genero is your *husband*? *The* Luigi Genero?"

"Yes," Dani's expression screamed undiluted terror. Her hands spread protectively over her baby bump.

I slumped back in my seat, all synapses firing. Courtesy of my dad, I'd grown up around crooks. I was familiar with the seedy underbelly of Dublin and London and the slimy creatures who inhabited that world. Even by Dad's low standards, the Genero gang was notorious. They were a branch of the Italian Mafia and had their grubby fingers in every illicit pie in London. The head of the gang was a guy called Gio

Genero. Gio had eight sons, each more vicious than the last. Luigi was the youngest and scariest of the bunch.

"I had the misfortune to run across Luigi in a former life." A life I'd happily left behind. "I take it you and Del are on the run?"

Dani swallowed audibly and dabbed at her eyes with a tissue. "My uncle owns Villa Margherita. Which is to say, his company owns it. He keeps this place for his use when he needs it. He's allowing us to stay here until the baby is born." Her olive skin had lost its sickly green tinge, but her eyes were large with fright. "We have to find Jimmy. They'll hurt him. And then they'll hurt me and the baby."

I wanted to reassure her, but it would've been a lie. For all we knew, my brother was already dead. At that thought, a wave of nausea threatened to undo my feigned calm. I shifted my attention to Dani's bump. Having once used a fake baby belly as a disguise, I was aware of how much a pregnancy predisposed people to be sympathetic. While I was confident Dani's pregnancy was the real deal, I didn't know her, and I couldn't trust her—at least, not yet.

"Is the baby Del's?"

A flicker of annoyance crossed her face. "Of course. That's why we ran. As soon as I had my first scan, Luigi would've known the baby couldn't be his."

"Sorry, but I had to ask. If you were carrying Luigi's child, the situation would be messy."

Her brow arched. "I got pregnant by his chauffeur. Trust me, the situation is plenty messy."

I couldn't see Del being anyone's chauffeur. Getaway driver, maybe—if they were desperate. What role had Del truly played in the Genero gang?

I forced myself to focus on the here and now. "If Del changed his name to Jimmy, I assume Dani isn't your real name."

"I'm Anna-Sofia," she whispered. "But we're careful to call each other by our new names, even when we're alone. Less chance of slipping up in public. Can you please call me Dani? Like I said, Jocelyn eavesdrops."

"Sure. Let's stick to Dani and Jimmy." I grimaced. "And Kimmy, I suppose."

The mention of my ridiculous, rhyming twin name brought a brief smile to Dani's lips. Then her eyes clouded over again. "I don't know what to do. If Luigi's found Jimmy—"

"The guy who threatened me on the phone wasn't Luigi," I interjected. "I've met Luigi Genero. Unless he tells you he's Italian, you wouldn't know from speaking to him. Plus, his English accent reeks of expensive schools. The guy who answered my brother's phone was older and has spent time in the East End of London. His English is excellent, but he speaks with a hint of an Italian accent."

She waved her tissue in a dismissive gesture. "Luigi has contacts all over Italy."

"Right. Presumably, the dude on the phone is one such contact. If Luigi's minions have D—Jimmy—it's only a matter of time before they find you. You have to leave the villa."

Dani's chin jutted in defiance. "Jimmy would never betray me. He'd die before giving up our address."

I had far less faith in my weasel brother's ability to withstand five minutes of torture, but I let it slide. "If Luigi's people captured Jimmy in Monterosso, it won't take them long to find you. I got your address within five minutes of arriving in town. I strolled into an ice cream parlor and met your neighbor Barbie."

Dani's head shot up. "Jimmy didn't give you this address?"

"You read his messages. All he gave me was a cryptic mention of our childhood hideout. And trust me, that looked nothing like this place."

She digested this information for a moment, then shook her head. "I'm not running away. Not without Jimmy. We have to rescue him. We can't leave him with those people. As soon as he finds out where I'm staying, Luigi will have him killed and then come for me."

"You're about to pop, Dani. *We* will do nothing. *I'll* do my best to find my brother and keep you both safe." Confiding in the cops flashed through my mind, but I dismissed it mid-thought. The Generos had cops on their payroll in London. I had to assume Italy was no different.

Dani's dark eyes bored into me, and the defiant jut of her chin was back. "How will you find Jimmy? Do you even know your way around Cinque Terre?"

"No, but it's a relatively small area and I have a map app." There was also the hairy possibility that my brother was no longer in the vicinity. In a fast car, his captors could've taken him far away by now. "Barbie mentioned my brother had a Vespa. Could I borrow it?"

"Jimmy *had* a Vespa." A flash of raw anger passed over Dani's face. "Last week, he wrecked it by driving it into the sea on a drunken bet."

*Ouch.* "A typical Del move," I said in sympathy. "Are you sure you want to have a baby with my brother?"

Dani jabbed her enormous belly. "It's a little late to have second thoughts, don't you think?"

"Fair point."

She sat back in her chair and stared at me challengingly. "Jimmy mentions you're a P.I. in one of his messages to you. Is this true?"

"I've solved a few mysteries, yes," I hedged, not wanting to reveal the extent of my inexperience. "Do you have anywhere else to stay? With the uncle who owns this place, for example?"

Dani's headshake was emphatic. "No way. I don't

want to put him and his family in danger. He's already taking a colossal risk letting us live here."

"What about friends who'd be willing to help?"

Her eyes dropped to her stomach. "Luigi isolated me from my former life. I don't have friends anymore."

I got it. I'd survived an abusive relationship. My ex had taken pleasure in ensuring I had no one to run to when his seeming adoration had taken a dark turn. And the worst part? I'd let him. Yes, any therapist worth having would dispute my culpability in my own abuse, but humiliation and self-flagellation were hard habits to kick.

"Can't you think of anywhere you could go?" I pressed. "If I'm out looking for my brother, you'll be on your own. Do you want to take that risk?"

"Of course not, but what choice do I have?" Dani exhaled sharply. "Look, I've had a difficult pregnancy. I was on bed rest until a couple of weeks ago. I'm allowed to move around a little now, but I'm in constant pain."

The word combo of 'pain' and 'pregnancy' skyrocketed me into a nightmare vision in which I was forced to deliver Dani's baby.

Catching my horrified expression, she added, "Don't panic. I have SPD—symphysis pubis dysfunction. In layperson's terms, my pubic bones move around too much. It should go away after the baby's born."

"Will you need to have a...? What do you call it? C-section?" Not having friends with kids, my knowledge of childbirth was limited to biology lessons and dramatic soap opera deliveries.

"Yes, I'll have a C-section, but for other reasons. I'm scheduled to go to the hospital on Friday." A spasm of pain crossed Dani's face. "We need to find Jimmy. I don't want to give birth alone."

At her mention of the hospital, an idea struck me. "Couldn't you fake an emergency and get admitted to the hospital early? You'd be safe there."

"Seriously?" Dani gave me a withering look. "The hospital in Levanto is a small general hospital. They don't have armed guards at the door. I'm safer here. I have Bernice, and there's always someone around. Even Jocelyn would defend me in an emergency."

I opened my mouth to argue that one overly friendly dog and one overly weird neighbor didn't represent a pro protection team. But where else could she go? I couldn't watch over her 24/7 if I was out looking for my brother.

"See what I mean?" Dani demanded, correctly reading my thoughts. "The villa is the safest place I can be at the moment, especially with this by my side." She stuck her hand in between the cushions of her armchair and withdrew an automatic pistol.

I let out a low whistle. Italy's gun laws were strict. No way did Dani have a license for that beauty. "So you have a gun. Great. So will they—*plural*. The villa is the first place they'll look for you once Del coughs up the address."

"Call him Jimmy. And he won't tell them where we live."

"I wish I could believe that. Staying here is lunacy, Dani. You'd be putting yourself and everyone who lives here in danger." Harsh, but true, and it had to be said.

A look of utter bleakness flashed across her face before she shuttered her emotions. "This is my home. It's the first place I've felt safe since I married Luigi."

"This apartment feeling like home won't transform it into a fortress. Can't you see how vulnerable you are here?"

"Yes, of course. I'm not stupid." She sounded angry, frustrated, and scared. "If I had a safe place to go, I'd have left already."

The woman was infuriating. Why was she adamant about staying at the villa? Did she truly have nowhere else to go, or was she spinning me a yarn? First chance I got, I'd dig for info on Anna-Sofia Genero. Right now, I didn't have time to keep arguing with her. "Okay, but if you stay here, you need to act normal. If Luigi's people found my brother, you don't want to draw attention to yourself. What do you usually do on a Sunday evening?"

"Attend a potluck dinner with my neighbors. Even while I was on bed rest, I could do that. Everyone was so kind. I always had a place to lie down."

"So go to tonight's dinner."

"You should come, too. Guests are welcome."

"I don't have time to party," I said with a touch of impatience. "I need to look for Jimmy, remember?"

"Then come by when you get back." At my skeptical expression, she added, "It'd look weird if you didn't show, especially now that Barbie knows you're visiting. Saul and Riccardo are this week's hosts. They live across from Jocelyn."

"Lucky Saul and Riccardo," I said dryly, glancing at my watch. "I want to go down to town to ask if anyone saw Del between him leaving Marco's place and the time he sent me the message."

"You're more likely to get that answer tomorrow morning," Dani said. "Life in Monterosso works in shifts. The early morning crowd doesn't cross paths with the evening revelers."

"It's worth a try. I have no other leads. Can you at least give me the contact details for Marco and the other people my brother was with last night? Maybe they heard or saw something out of the ordinary."

"Sure. I don't have all their numbers, but I can give you Marco's and Alessandro's."

Dani found the numbers on her phone and I copied them into my contacts, along with Dani's number and Marco's address.

"But you won't find him at home now," she added. "He's a waiter at La Cantina del Pescatore in the old town. He usually works Sunday evenings."

"What about work colleagues? Where's my brother working these days?"

Dani's embarrassed flush answered that question. She twisted a ring on her finger—a classy ruby that my brother could never afford.

"Jimmy's between jobs at the moment," she said, not meeting my eye. "Sometimes, he helps on Alessandro's uncle's fishing boat. That's where he was last night before he went out with the boys."

The idea of Del-slash-Jimmy dealing with fish struck a comical note. I had a flashback to my infofest on Cinque Terre on the drive down. All the tiny inlets along the Italian Riviera made it a popular place for smugglers. What dodgy deals was my brother involved in this time? What if his current predicament had nothing to do with Dani's ex and everything to do with Del once again getting mixed up with the wrong crowd?

I pocketed my phone and stood, taking a giant step over the dog. "Marco's restaurant will open soon. I want to catch him before he's busy."

Bernice got to her paws and whined, fixing her pleading, puppy-dog eyes first on me, and then on Dani.

"Would you mind taking Bernice with you?" Dani asked. "She's way overdue for a walk. Jimmy takes her because I can't at the moment, and seeing as Jimmy isn't here..."

She trailed off, leaving loaf-sized breadcrumbs of guilt for me to follow.

I regarded the oversized furball with trepidation. "You want me to take a dog on an investigation?"

"She'll help you blend in. Won't you, Bernice?" Dani leaned down and scratched the dog's neck. "Her leash is hanging by the door, along with spare poop bags."

"Poop bags?" I invested the words with due horror. "I didn't sign up for poop bags."

I hadn't signed up for any of this, come to think of it. I was supposed to be on my way to Florida.

The mention of poop bags had a galvanizing effect on Bernice. She raced to the door, tugged on the handle, and howled.

"See?" Dani cast me the limpet gaze that had surely lured countless idiot males to their doom.

"Whatever," I grumbled. "Don't you want me to find Jimmy before midnight? The dog will slow me down."

"I wouldn't be so sure. Bernice moves fast."

"Fantastic," I said, not bothering to hide my sarcasm. "I'll spend my time chasing a dog instead of looking for my kidnapped brother. Makes total sense."

I made to move, but Dani grabbed my arm and dropped her voice to a whisper. "Thank you, Angel. I don't know what I'd have done if you hadn't shown up today."

"Don't thank me until I've tracked down my

brother." I was half-tempted to ask her for the pistol, but dismissed the idea. The last thing I needed was to get nicked by the cops for illegal possession of a firearm. With me locked up, Del would be on his own.

Dani waddled down to the door and clipped a leash onto Bernice's collar. She handed me the leash and a handful of the dreaded poop bags.

"How in the world did you and my brother wind up with a dog? Surely she's inconvenient in your current condition?"

Dani's nose twitched. "Jimmy won her in a game of poker."

"My brother playing poker comes as no surprise, but actually winning?" I snorted. "Not a chance."

Dani cracked a minuscule smile. "I assume Bernice's previous owner wanted to get rid of her and recognized Jimmy as an easy mark." Her gaze grew wistful. "I don't suppose you'd like to take her home with you?"

"I have two housemates and one housecat. I doubt any of them would welcome Bernice into our happy home."

"Ah, well," Dani said philosophically. "It was worth a try."

## 6

*I* needn't have worried about the dog slowing me down. The instant I shut the villa's gates, Bernice shot down the road, yanking free of my grip on her leash.

"Stop," I yelled. "Bad dog."

Bernice ignored me, forcing me into a sprint. She bounded down the steep slope, past lush villas, precariously parked cars, and a procession of increasingly irate cyclists. Bernice never broke her stride. I staggered after the dog, coming to an ungainly halt at the foot of the slope where the suburbs met the beach.

Bernice had found a new playmate. One of the bodysurfers I'd spotted earlier was fleeing down the sand with Bernice nipping at his wetsuit-clad backside. I swore loudly in several languages, earning me a reproachful glare from an older woman and her grandchildren.

I scanned my surroundings, searching for inspiration. It came in the form of a basketball. A group of preteens played on the court next to the beach. I pulled out my wallet, checked my cash situation, and waved a crisp fifty-euro note at them. "The ball," I gasped in Italian. "I'll give you fifty for that ball."

"Forget it, lady," replied a sullen kid with a mop of hair on top and badly shaven sides. "We want to play."

I reached into my purse again and discovered an extra fiver. "How about fifty-five?"

The boy snorted and turned his back on me. At his age, I'd have happily parted with my beat-up skateboard for fifty-five quid. Was inflation to blame? While I pondered this important economic question, an apple-cheeked preschooler sidled over to me.

"You can have my ball for fifty-five." She held out a grubby ball decorated with daisies.

I was being fleeced, but I was desperate. "Deal."

Transaction completed, I took the ball and ran down to the beach. Bernice was chasing her new friend in circles while his body-surfing companion tried to catch her by the collar. I put two fingers to my lips and whistled. Then I threw the ball in Bernice's direction.

She barked in delight and shot off after the ball. Assuming I was Bernice's owner, the body surfers hurled abuse at me. I flipped them the bird and kept walking.

When I caught up with Bernice, she was burying her new ball in the sand. I grabbed the end of her leash and tugged. To my amazement, she looked up, barked a greeting, and sat obediently at my feet. I eyed her with suspicion. "Why are you so well-behaved all of a sudden?"

She panted and batted her large doggy eyes at me.

"Food, huh? If we track down Del's pal Marco, I'll buy you a sausage." I scooped up the ball and urged her into a trot.

Except for an incident involving a scooter in the tunnel that led to the old town, Bernice behaved beautifully. My phone's maps app led me past the path up to the Aurora Tower, part of the ancient fortress that had once protected Monterosso. In the hills above the old town, the remains of the Fieschi Castle were visible. On the other side of the tunnel, we swerved past the small marina and headed toward the charming but labyrinthine streets of Monterosso.

The streets—more like narrow alleyways—were pedestrian-only apart from scooters and Piaggio Apes—those three-wheeled microvans beloved by Italians. The alleyways wound up at a sharp incline. Some had steps, including a flight of steps that led up to a Capuchin monastery. When Bernice and I turned into one of the identikit narrow alleyways, a prickling on the nape of my neck made me spin around. A couple of baseball-capped tourists peered into a shop window. A middle-aged man strolled by, arm in arm with a much younger companion.

I breathed out. What was wrong with me? No one was following me. Or were they? Was the persistent sensation that I was being watched not a result of my sleep-deprived paranoia? Were the people who had Jimmy following me? If so, had I led Luigi Genero's thugs to the villa?

Bernice whined and tugged on her leash, reminding me I had a purpose, and that purpose relied on me not losing my mind.

I found the restaurant where Marco worked after getting lost twice. The place had opened for the dinner crowd, and it was just warm enough for some of the hardier diners to sit outside. I didn't need to find Marco. Bernice did the job for me. A stocky guy of around thirty emerged from the back of the restaurant, carrying a tray of appetizers. Bernice zoomed toward him, encircling his legs with an enthusiastic whoop.

Marco kept hold of the tray and raised it out of Bernice's reach. When she showed distinct signs of leaping up, I surged forward and grabbed her by the collar. "Sorry about that," I said in Italian. "She's a bit of a handful."

"No harm, no foul. Bernice gets excited." Marco grinned down at me. "With that hair, no need to ask who you are. Jimmy never said his sister was in town."

"He didn't know I'd be in town. Listen, do you have a sec? It's about Jimmy."

Marco inclined his head, seemingly incurious about his friend's sister showing up at his place of work unannounced. "Sure. Let me serve this food and I'll be right with you."

A couple of minutes later, Marco and I sat at an indoor table, a carafe of wine between us, Bernice and a bowl of meat at our feet. The wine was at Marco's insistence, and I suspected he was engaging in a touch of hair of the dog after last night's shenanigans.

He clinked his wineglass against mine and treated me to a lothario look. "If Jimmy wants to play matchmaker, why didn't he come along to introduce you to me?"

Ah, so that was why Marco had taken my visit in his stride. Should I feel flattered or indignant? "Put a lid on your Italian libido. Besides, I was under the impression that my brother was banned from every establishment in Monterosso."

Marco's smile turned into a genuine grin. "True, but I sneak him in here if the boss isn't around. No offence, but if Jimmy didn't send you, why are you here?"

"For information. What time did Jimmy leave your place this morning?"

Marco drummed his fingers on the tabletop. "I dunno. Six? Six-thirty? He wanted to get home before Dani woke up. She hates him being gone, you know? Very possessive."

I ignored this swipe at my brother's very pregnant

girlfriend. I had my own doubts about Dani, but I didn't care to discuss them with Marco. "Did you see Jimmy leave?"

"Nah. I heard him bumbling about and just yelled goodbye and went back to sleep." A line appeared between his brows. "Why all these questions?"

"My brother never made it home after he left your place this morning."

If this information surprised Marco, he didn't show it. "So Jimmy met a friend, got an opportunity to make a bit of cash. It happens."

"I'm sure it happens," I said, my tone sandpaper dry, "and I can well imagine what sort of cash-making opportunities come my brother's way. But that's not what happened today. He sent me panicked text messages, begging me to come to Monterosso. When I got here, I called his number and a strange man answered. Made threats. Do you know anything about this?"

His nonchalance ebbed a tad. "Made threats? Who made threats?"

"I don't know. He didn't give a name." I paused, watching Marco's face. "Dani suggested he might be her ex."

Marco cocked his head to one side, considering my words. "Jimmy mentioned they'd left England to get away from Dani's ex."

Either he was an excellent actor, or my brother

hadn't divulged Dani's ex's identity. "Can you think of any other candidates who'd threaten my brother?"

This got a reaction. Marco shifted in his seat, suddenly finding his wineglass fascinating. "You know Jimmy. He has a knack for upsetting people."

"Who's he upset recently?" I made a wild guess. "The so-called fishermen?"

Marco sat forward, his eyes darting from side to side. "Shh. Do you want to get your brother in trouble?"

"My brother's already in trouble. I need to know who with and where to find them."

Marco took a long drink of wine before answering. "Jimmy did a few jobs for Paolo Moretti. I hear Paolo wasn't happy with Jimmy's...work ethic."

I rolled my eyes. "What jobs?"

Marco avoided my gaze. "This and that."

"Of the buying and selling variety? With an emphasis on the selling part?"

"Something along those lines." Marco spread his palms wide. "Look, I don't get involved. I work at my uncle's restaurant, and I mind my business about what other people do to earn their crust."

I'd met guys like Marco before. Smooth-talking, wise-cracking, and lie-telling. I was no connoisseur, but Marco hadn't purchased the fancy watch on his wrist on a small-town waiter's salary.

"Where can I find Paolo Moretti?"

Marco's head shook emphatically. "No way. Moretti's not the sort of person you want to find."

"Then he's exactly the sort of person I'm looking for. Are you going to give me his address or do I need to scream the place down about you wearing a contraband watch?"

Marco muttered under his breath. "You can scream about contraband all you want. You think anyone cares? If you're determined to find Moretti, he usually hangs out at Pepe's bar on Via Fegina."

I took a sip of my wine—a more-than-decent white —and stood. "Thanks for the info, Marco. Come on, Bernice. Time to go."

The dog licked her bowl clean and followed me out of the restaurant. We wound our way through the old town and back to the street facing the beach.

Pepe's bar turned out to be a few doors down from Arturo's ice cream parlor. When I barged in, the hum of conversation fell to a hush. It didn't take long to figure out why. I was the only person under the age of sixty, and one of the few women in the joint. Bernice had the dubious distinction of being the only dog.

A burly barman emerged from behind the counter. "Get that dog off my premises. She's banned. She eats furniture."

"You know Bernice?"

"Know her?" His nostrils quivered. "I used to own her. I'm still repairing my house after she ran amok."

"Ah. You must be the dude who lost her to my brother in a game of poker."

A chorus of laughter around the bar framed the man's grin. "Lost? Sure. Jimmy can keep telling himself that." The grin faded. "He's also banned, by the way."

"I'm happy to remove Bernice from your bar. However, I want to have a word with one of your patrons first. Can you point out Paolo Moretti?"

The barman's neck gave an involuntary jerk to the left. "He's not in yet."

"Bullshit." I checked out the row of guys propping up the bar. Only one still had his back to me. A familiar back—a slither of unease snaked down my spine. "Come on, Bernice. Let's say hello to one of your old friends. Which one's Paolo?"

Bernice barked, tugged on her leash, and dragged me across the room. She stopped in front of the barstool occupied by the gray-haired, gray-clothed man who'd played chess with Arturo earlier.

"Mr. Moretti? May I have a word with you?"

The man turned slowly to face me. He looked like a suburban grandfather—bland and unassuming. An instinct honed by a lifetime surrounded by thugs told me differently.

"I don't like the English," he said in heavily accented English.

"In that case," I replied in Italian, "it's just as well I'm not English."

His lips quivered with what might have been amusement, but he made no response.

I got straight to the point. "I'm looking for my brother Jimmy. He used to work for you."

Silence reigned in the room, and I felt several pairs of eyes bore into my back.

Paolo Moretti took a sip from his wineglass and gave me a long stare. "I know Jimmy, but he doesn't work for me."

"I heard different."

"Then you heard wrong. Jimmy did a job or two for me, but we parted ways." Moretti drew back his lips into a rictus of a smile. "Sorry, I can't be more help."

"If my brother doesn't work for you anymore, any idea who he's working for?"

The man gave a deceptively lazy half-shrug. "Don't know, don't care. I don't like people keeping tabs on me, and I don't keep tabs on people."

A man like Moretti would know everything about everyone, but I didn't want to antagonize him any more than I already had. Maybe Dani's pregnancy would soften him. Didn't Italians have a reputation for loving babies?

"My brother's girlfriend is about to have their first child. I need to find him. Surely you don't want her to give birth alone?"

"Not my problem, sweetheart." Moretti jerked a thumb at the door. "Now get that dog out of my boozer."

I slunk out of the bar, down, but not defeated. Did Moretti's hostility mean he was hiding something? Or had he simply taken against my brother and, by extension, me?

Back on the street, I evaluated my options. I had Del's friend Alessandro's phone number, but no address. Also, Dani had mentioned Del working on Alessandro's uncle's fishing boat. Assuming my brother hadn't worked for multiple fishermen, this implied Alessandro's uncle was Paolo Moretti. Would the nephew prove more forthcoming with information?

Another option was to do the rounds of the local bars. Del was memorable, given his tendency to get thrown out of drinking establishments. Perhaps someone would provide a clue as to who Del had upset recently. Knowing him, it'd be a long list.

Bernice tugged on her leash, showing signs of making another break for freedom. I took the hint and started moving. She made a beeline for the beach, squatted down, and did her business.

While Bernice was otherwise occupied, I tried Alessandro's number.

It went straight to voicemail.

"Hey, Alessandro. This is Kimmy..." Why hadn't I thought to ask Dani what fake surname Del was using? "I'm Jimmy's sister. He's gone AWOL, and Dani and I are worried. Can you call me back? Thanks."

I pocketed the phone, bagged the poop, and escorted Bernice back down the strand. I figured the sea air might inspire me with a solution to the Missing Brother problem. The closer we got to the parking lot end of the beach, the more Bernice picked up steam. I wished I could say the same for me.

When my phone buzzed with an incoming call, my blood pressure skyrocketed. I fumbled for the phone. Dani's name flashed on the screen. "Dani?" I asked the instant I hit connect. "Have you found him?"

Her voice broke on a sob. "You need to come back to the villa. I got a ransom note shoved under the door. They want twenty-five thousand euros, or they'll kill Jimmy."

## 7

*I* stagger-ran through Monterosso, allowing Bernice to pull me most of the way. While my legs moved, my mind whirled. None of this made sense. I'd assumed my brother's kidnapping was connected to Dani's violent ex, Luigi Genero. The ransom demand put a spoke in that theory.

If Luigi's muscled minions were holding Del captive, their priority would be using him to track down Dani. However, the ransom note was slipped under Dani's door, meaning its sender knew exactly where she lived. Which wasn't a huge surprise. It had taken me five minutes in Monterosso to find the villa's address, and I was working with far less info than Luigi's thugs would have at their disposal. How hard could it be to find the dwelling of one red-haired Irishman and his heavily pregnant girlfriend?

I paused at the end of Via Fegina to catch my

breath. Apart from Luigi, who had a reason to hold my brother hostage? Paolo Moretti? He had the pervading air of menace beloved by small-scale crooks. He'd admitted my brother had done a couple of jobs for him, and that they'd since "parted ways." Had Del cheated Paolo or stolen from him? That might explain the ransom demand.

Bernice yanked on the leash, and I braced myself for the brutal climb to Villa Margherita. When I'd last seen the road leading up to the villa, it had been dusk. Now the sky was an inky black, and the temperature had plummeted. Somehow, the dark and the cold made the road appear even steeper. This was especially apparent when the dog took off up the hill. Unless I wanted to deal with a runaway puppy on top of all the other craziness, I had no option but to keep up with her punishing pace.

Thirty seconds into our ascent, my legs ached, and my chest worked overtime. I wanted to slump against the nearest bush, but I didn't trust Bernice not to use the opportunity to make another break for freedom, leaving me to explain her disappearance to Dani. While I wasn't a fitness freak, my current exhaustion was the result of my action-packed weekend in Switzerland. My body was covered in bruises, and I hadn't slept properly in days.

I hauled air into my lungs and gave myself a mental pep talk. It wasn't much further to the villa. It had taken me less than twenty minutes to walk there earlier. Moving at this speed, I'd arrive in ten. I could survive ten more minutes of running, right?

As a distraction from my burning lungs and limbs, I concentrated on the Del dilemma. Given my brother's shambolic employment history as a lackey for various London gangsters, who knew how many people had a motive for his kidnap? There was only one person who sprang to mind, and he was the last man I wanted to contact—Dad.

Red-hot rage seared through me at the mere thought of my father. What sort of parent sided with their daughter's violent boyfriend, simply because said boyfriend was his gangster boss's son? Noel Doyle, apparently.

Gosh, I missed Sidney. He'd talk me off the ledge and make sure I did nothing crazy. Part of me—a *big* part of me—regretted not telling him about Del's message. Sidney would've insisted on accompanying me to Italy. Which was why I'd kept my lips zipped. But if he were here, he could help me figure out my next move.

Who else could I ask for help? The Omega Group? The instant my mother learned I hadn't caught the flight to Florida, she'd refuse to let anyone on the team come to my aid. After all, Del wasn't her son. He was merely her ex-stepson from several marriages ago.

What about Luc? Funny how I'd barely thought of Luc since he'd said goodbye to Sidney and me yesterday evening. Since we'd first met in July, he'd had a tendency to creep into my thoughts, however hard I tried to shut them down. Leaving my feelings for the man aside, he was ex-military and an experienced P.I. He'd know what to do in this situation.

But would Luc be prepared to go behind my mother's back? I wasn't so sure. Besides, he'd been injured during our Swiss adventure. He was probably resting at home on a wave of heavy-duty pain meds.

When Villa Margherita came into view, Bernice gave a *woof* of excitement and increased her speed. Clearly, this dog had a touch of the homing pigeon. Or perhaps the scent of barbecue reminded her it had been at least twenty minutes since her last meal.

This time, I hit every doorbell on the gate. One of them, surely, would let us in. Music and laughter floated down from upstairs, but no one reacted to my incessant ringing. I dropped to my haunches and tickled Bernice. "Come on, girl. You love to bark. Don't you want some of that freshly grilled meat? Give me a nice, high-pitched howl."

Bernice wagged her tail, lolled her tongue, and licked the fifty-five-euro rip-off ball I still clutched under one arm. At that instant, a cat strolled along the wall of the villa. Scenting a feline foe, Bernice emitted a blood-curdling growl. The cat hissed, arched its back, and yowled.

This was the sign Bernice had been waiting for. She leaped at the wall, sending the cat flying. Dog and cat engaged in an ear-bleeding cacophony of howling and yowling. Upstairs, the music stopped, followed by the sound of feet on gravel. The gate slid open to reveal Barbie, from Arturo's ice cream parlor, next to Jocelyn Dingus-Cockett.

Ignoring social etiquette, Bernice charged through the gate and shot off in pursuit of the cat.

Jocelyn glowered at me. "She's scaring Persephone."

"Forget the cat," I snapped. "Where's Dani?"

"She's upstairs at the potluck." Barbie regarded me with a curious expression. "What happened to you? You didn't look this...disheveled...when I saw you a couple of hours ago."

I jabbed a finger in the direction Bernice had headed. "That dog happened. She dragged me all over Monterosso at turbo speed."

Jocelyn gave a gleeful snort and turned to Barbie. "What have I been saying since the day Jimmy moved that creature into the villa? That dog is a public nuisance. Jimmy won't control her, and Dani can't."

Barbie's lips twitched. "Bernice doesn't mean any harm. She's just a puppy."

I glanced up at the balcony on the third floor, where a group was now gathered, watching Bernice cavort among the flower beds in search of the cat. "What does Dani usually do with the dog when she goes to the weekly potluck? I assume Bernice isn't welcome."

"Depends on who's hosting," Barbie said. "This

week, it's Saul and Riccardo's turn. They're fine with Bernice tagging along. Jocelyn and I are on our way to get more ice from the basement. Saul and Riccardo live on the top floor. First door to the right. Why don't you go on up and join the party?"

I opened my mouth to protest that the last thing I wanted to do was party, but I caught sight of Dani peering down over the balcony. I needed to talk to her about the ransom demand. While I was relieved to see she'd taken my advice and attended the weekly dinner, we'd have to find an excuse to talk one to one.

I whistled for the dog to join me. Bernice, having lost sight and scent of the cat, bounded over to me and up the stone steps. Exhausted from my forced runs up and down the hill, I followed at a more sedate pace. Every limb ached. Every item of clothing stuck to my body. I wanted a bath and a bed. But with my brother held captive by goodness knew who, I was unlikely to get either.

When I reached the outdoor landing, the door leading to the hallway that separated the two top floor apartments was ajar. Bernice was already inside the building, whining at an open door. I squinted and fumbled for a light switch. My fingers skimmed the stone wall but met no switch. Which apartment was hosting the party? Had Barbie said left or right?

Light spilled under both doors. As I grew closer, the source of the music was obviously coming from my right, but Bernice seemed determined to access the apartment opposite.

I tried to grab her collar. "Oh, no, you don't. You can't sneak into people's homes uninvited."

As was her custom, Bernice ignored me. She nudged the door open with her muzzle and shot inside. A human exclamation of protest sounded from within, followed by feline yowling. Bracing myself for a well-deserved telling-off, I sighed and stepped inside. Waves of heat hit me. Whoever lived here liked their environment on the sauna-side of toasty.

I followed the sound of Bernice's excited barking. "I'm sorry," I called in Italian, not wanting to alarm the occupant any further. "She barged in before I could stop her."

I reached a living room stuffed with shabby furniture. And then my breath caught, my stomach roiled, and my toes recoiled so much my nails practically cut into my soles.

In front of a blazing fire, a naked man lay spreadeagled across a sheepskin rug, a poker protruding from his back.

And standing over him, with blood-stained hands, was Sidney.

*a*fter the shock-filled weekend Sidney and I had just spent in the Swiss Alps, I should've been unfazed. Turned out the sight of a murdered man still had the power to reduce me to a goggle-eyed, jelly-kneed, babbling mess. My panic ebbed when I saw the hair—jet-black and straight, not red and curly. The dead man wasn't my brother.

I dragged my attention away from the corpse and stared into Sidney's shell-shocked face. "What happened? Who's the dead dude?"

My friend's gaze dropped to the body, and an expression of revulsion contorted his face. "I don't know who he is or who killed him. I found his body a couple of minutes before you and the dog arrived."

"Why are you here, Sidney? You're supposed to be on your way to Florida."

His head jerked up, and the look in his eyes was

accusatory. "So were you. Instead, you abandoned me and hightailed it to Italy. Why did you come to Monterosso, Angel? Did it have to do with the dead man?"

"No. At least, I don't think so."

Before Sidney had the chance to demand more details, Bernice spied another cat cowering behind a dilapidated sofa. With a delighted *woof*, the dog raced over to her new playmate. The cat hissed, darted out of Bernice's way, and scrambled up the bookshelves that lined the living room walls.

I counted four cats on those shelves, all positioned high enough to evade Bernice. They were in various stages of indignation that a dog had invaded their home. The ginger tabby that Bernice had just routed out of its hiding place arched its back and bared its teeth. The Persian lounging in front of a row of Charles Dickens novels exuded haughty disdain. A tortoiseshell of indeterminate lineage had curled up for a snooze. And the Seal Point Siamese that nestled on a shelf of political tomes regarded the action below with disinterest.

The temperature was hotter than Hades. Sweat beaded under my jacket. I unzipped it and rolled up my sweater sleeves. "Whoever lives in this apartment must be part lizard."

Sidney snorted. "Whoever lives in this apartment is a bona fide fruit cake. Have you seen their whiteboard?"

"Not yet." I surveyed the room. To the right of the open fire stood a large whiteboard. Photos, maps, and sticky notes cluttered every centimeter. It looked like a comic book hero's version of a murder board.

"Do you think our corpse created that board?" Sidney asked. "And could it have anything to do with his death?"

"If we knew who the dead man was, we might have a clue." I abandoned my perusal of the whiteboard and eyed my friend with suspicion. "Sidney, how did you find me? There's no way you could have hired a car in time to follow me. I drive fast."

A smug smirk stretched across his face. "Easy. I bribed the bloke in the car rental office. He let me access your car's tracking data. All I had to do was hire another car and follow your lead."

My mouth gaped. "I'm not sure whether to be horrified or impressed," I said once I'd gotten over the initial shock. "A few months ago, you didn't even know your laptop could trace your phone. And now here you are tracking me all the way to Italy."

Giving up on the cats, Bernice had turned her attention to the dead body. She sniffed it, threw back her head, and let out the most blood-curdling, ear-splitting noise I'd ever encountered. Bernice's keening jolted the cats out of their studied hauteur. They began a literal cat's chorus, melding their voices with the dog's, creating a cacophony of tinnitus-inducing proportions.

Unsurprisingly, the racket ended our conversation and drew the attention of the villa's other occupants. Thirty seconds after the din began, an outraged Jocelyn stalked into the room, armed with attitude and a toilet brush. Holding the toilet brush like a knight brandishes a sword, he stopped short at the sight of Bernice, whose bulk shielded the body from view.

The man's lips retracted in a grimace. "I don't allow that dog in my apartment. She terrorizes my cats."

This was Jocelyn's place? Okay, that made sense. He was the type to have a murder board. And he'd mentioned having several cats. But although he was an oddball, he didn't strike me as the sort of bloke who went around collecting corpses.

Before I could interrogate Jocelyn about his deceased visitor, he caught sight of my friend. "*Sidney?*"

"*Jocelyn?*" Sidney goggled at him. "I thought you were in an underground bolthole in Nevada, researching Area 51 conspiracy theories."

Jocelyn scratched his sideburns. "You're behind the times," he yelled over the animals' racket. "Area 51 was last year's book. I've moved on to Mafia alien conspiracies."

Mafia alien conspiracies? The guy was a complete loon.

Sidney turned to me with the dour expression I

associate with funeral directors and debt collectors. "Jocelyn's my second cousin."

"First cousin once removed," Jocelyn corrected. "But we're not close. We see each other at extended family events. Weddings. Funerals. Aunt Edith's séances."

"Your aunt holds séances?" My voice had a croaky quality. If we didn't get the dog and cats to stop making noise, I'd lose my ability to speak after all this shouting. "Strike that question. And scratch the catch-up. There's a dead man on your living room floor, Jocelyn. Care to shed light on the matter?"

Jocelyn's lower jaw had a fight with gravity, and gravity won. "What dead man?"

I nudged Bernice to move. Still maintaining her vocal vigil, she shifted to the left, giving Jocelyn an unimpeded view of the corpse.

He made a strangled choking noise. His grip on the handle loosened and the toilet brush fell onto the polished wooden floor with a clatter.

Sidney had somewhat recovered his composure. "Do you know who the man is?"

Jocelyn adjusted his orange-tinted spectacles. "He's face down on that awful rug. Do you expect me to identify him by his buttocks?"

A knock sounded on the door, barely audible over the animals. "Jocelyn?" Barbie called. "Are you okay in there? Did Bernice break into your apartment again?"

Jocelyn glared at me. "Yes," he roared. "Along with Jimmy's sister, my cousin, and, apparently, a corpse."

"What did you say?" Barbie yelled back. "A course?"

"Not a course," he shouted in response. "A corpse."

"We can't discuss anything with this noise," Sidney said to me. "Can you get the dog out of here?"

"I can try."

I grabbed Bernice's collar and urged her into motion. She went reluctantly, whining to get back to the dead man. I ignored her entreaties and escorted her out to the hall.

Barbie and a silver-haired man hovered outside Jocelyn's apartment. She'd swapped her cleavage-bearing uniform for a voluminous black dress that hung from her shoulders like an expensive garbage bag. The man looked like the sort of dude I'd expect to find at a pseudo-Eastern holistic retreat.

"What's going on in there?" Barbie demanded. "For a moment, I thought Jocelyn was talking about a corpse."

Her silver-haired companion smirked. "Don't be absurd. Jocelyn's weird, but he's not *that* weird."

The man's Australian accent was more refined than Barbie's. I judged him to be at least fifteen years older than her. Maybe closer to twenty. As a kid, I'd been criticized for my tendency to make snap judgements about people. Now that I was an adult, I knew those instinctual reactions were rarely wrong.

My gut told me this man was not a nice person. His blandly handsome features were set in a smug expression that I suspected was a near-permanent fixture. From his expertly gelled man bun to his eco-friendly linen suit and vegan leather shoes, he oozed the vainglory I associated with cult leaders and self-proclaimed philanthropists. I could totally see this man founding a religion.

Correctly deducing I was checking him out, but misinterpreting my motivation, the man stretched his lips into a self-satisfied smile. "I'm Ken, Barbie's significant other. You must be Jimmy's little sister, Kimmy. Dani's told me all about you."

How in the world had someone as nice as Barbie wound up with this dude? Was it the name? Did she harbor some kind of warped Barbie and Ken fantasy?

"If Dani told you all about me, it must have been a quick conversation. She and I met for the first time today." I pointed at the open door across the hall. "Is Dani in there? I need to speak to her."

Barbie twisted a strand of platinum hair around her index finger in what I soon learned was a habitual gesture. "She's resting on the sofa. That's why I volunteered to rescue Bernice from Jocelyn."

"Jocelyn would argue it's the opposite way around." I treated Ken to my own smug smile. "He was serious about the corpse, by the way."

Ken's polished veneer cracked beneath his deep tan. "No way."

Barbie let go of the hair around her finger with a snap and gawped at me. "Who's dead? Not someone from the villa?"

"I have no idea who the guy is or where he's from. Is anyone at the party a doctor? Or any kind of medical professional?"

"One of the women renting Number Five this week is a doctor," Barbie said. "Lucy, I think she's called. She and her sister haven't arrived yet, but I can go downstairs and fetch them."

"Perfect." I thrust Bernice's leash at a horrified Ken. "Bring Bernice to Dani and send Lucy to me. And one of you needs to call the cops."

A frown rippled across Barbie's forehead. "Why the cops? Don't you mean an ambulance?"

"We need to notify the police. The dead man was murdered."

I didn't wait for the inevitable horror and disbelief. Leaving them to deal with the dog, I slipped back inside Jocelyn's apartment and closed the door.

When I returned to the living room, Jocelyn had retrieved his toilet brush. The cats had lined up on the sofa, and the dead dude was still dead.

I pointed at the toilet brush. "Please tell me that isn't used."

"Of course not." Jocelyn sounded suitably indignant. "Riccardo asked me to fetch a new one from the supply cupboard in the basement. It's for their apartment. I thought I'd use it to lure the dog out of here. She enjoys playing tug."

Sidney was scrubbing the blood off his hands in the kitchen sink. "Did you call the police?" he asked over his shoulder. "They'll have to be informed."

"The neighbors are taking care of it."

"The police?" Jocelyn's voice rose in volume on that last syllable. "Why the police?"

I could sense my friend's struggle not to roll his eyes at his cousin.

"Because there's a man with a poker in his back lying dead in your living room," Sidney drawled. "Does his demise look accidental to you?"

"Can you think of a reason why I might not trust the police?" Jocelyn's had a high-pitched, breathy quality like he'd been hitting the helium hard. "You know why I hate the police."

My friend paled and shifted uncomfortably. "Yes. Sorry, man. I forgot. All the same, you must understand why we have to call them in this case."

Jocelyn blew a strand of greasy hair out of his face. "If you call them, what will happen to my research? The police will designate this room as a crime scene."

"It is a crime scene," I said, trying to catch Sidney's eye to give him a push to clue me in on what he and his cousin were referencing. "And the police will cordon off the entire apartment, not just this room."

"Then there's no time to lose." Jocelyn tossed the toilet brush onto an overstuffed armchair and launched himself at his whiteboard. "Don't just stand there, Kimmy. I need help."

Sidney dried his hands on a piece of kitchen towel. "Who's Kimmy?"

"I am." I shot him a warning look. "My brother calls me Kimmy instead of Kim, remember?"

It was a poor attempt at deflection, but Jocelyn didn't appear to notice. He was busy pulling photos, maps, and sticky notes off his board, and trying to keep them in some semblance of order. I was torn between helping him and ordering him to leave the board alone. What if the material he'd collected was connected to the murder?

I stared at the board, trying to memorize each note before it disappeared into the pile. A photo on the bottom row caught my eye and my breath hitched. "Hold on a sec." I grabbed Jocelyn's hand before he could remove the photo. "That's Luigi Genero."

"So?" Jocelyn yanked his hand free and added Luigi's photo to the pile. "Why do you care?"

"I care because Luigi Genero is mobbed up. Don't you think the cops will be interested in knowing why you have his photograph on that board?"

Jocelyn subjected me to a withering look. "Why do you think I'm removing it?"

"Are you writing about the Generos?" I demanded, my mental processor whirring. "Is that why you're in Monterosso?"

"Why would I come to Monterosso to research

Luigi Genero? The Generos are from Milan." He removed the last sticky note from the board and cast around for a container to store his precious notes.

I retrieved two leftover poop bags from my coat pocket and handed them to him. "Bernice needs oversized bags. This should be large enough to fit your research material."

Jocelyn snatched the bags without thanking me, dumped his stuff into one, and then grabbed a laptop from the coffee table. "You need to hide these for me."

Sidney and I exchanged a loaded look. "Absolutely not," I said. "I don't know you, and I don't know what this is all about."

A rap on the door silenced all of us. "That'll be the doctor who's attending the potluck. I asked Barbie to send her across."

Jocelyn scowled at me. "We can't let her in before I've removed my notes. I can't allow anyone else to see my research."

"What am I supposed to say to her? It'll look mighty suspicious if I refuse to let her in."

"Throw Jocelyn under a bus," Sidney suggested. "Tell her he fainted, and he's too embarrassed to see anyone until he's collected himself."

"That's a terrible excuse. She'll insist on checking he's okay."

"Then think of a better story." Sidney turned back to Jocelyn. "I can help you gather your research, but then what's the plan? Do you have a hiding place in mind?"

"Why are we helping him?" I demanded before Jocelyn could respond. "For all we know, he's the killer, and we're making ourselves accessories after the fact."

Not to mention the possibility that Jocelyn was involved in my brother's kidnapping. What were the odds of him having a photograph of Dani's ex on his board for any other reason? I needed to get Sidney alone—the sooner, the better.

A second rap sounded on the door, louder this time, more insistent. In the distance, sirens wailed. We were running out of time.

Sidney ran a hand through his thick mop of fair hair. "We can talk about this later, Angel. For now, please trust me when I say Jocelyn's no killer."

I regarded Sidney's cousin, who was racing around his apartment, grabbing papers and gadgets and stuffing them into poop bags. "Yeah, we need to talk, Sidney. About why you're here, why I'm here, and why your deranged cousin has a dead body in his apartment."

## 9

*L*eaving the men to gather the rest of Jocelyn's book research material, I tossed my jacket over the back of an armchair and strode to the door.

A crowd clustered in the hallway. Several faces stared back at me, agog with curiosity. A lady in her early forties sat in a wheelchair, sobbing into an old-fashioned handkerchief. A mousy woman of a similar age hovered beside her, patting her friend's arm in an ineffectual attempt to calm her down. Ken leaned against the wall, aiming for nonchalance but failing to conceal his glee. An anxious-looking Barbie had her arm around a weeping Dani's shoulders.

When she recognized me, Dani detached herself from Barbie, her enormous eyes wide with fear. "Is it Jimmy? Is he dead?"

"Not Jimmy. The dead man's older, skinnier, taller. Definitely not my brother."

She crumpled in relief, allowing Barbie to support her once again. "Thank goodness. When Ken said someone had been murdered, I panicked."

So had I. While I was glad my brother wasn't the corpse, I had an uneasy feeling he might be connected to the crime. A kidnapping and a murder on the same day couldn't be a coincidence, surely?

The mousy woman detached herself from her friend in the wheelchair. Lank brown hair threaded with gray framed a plain moon face. Her shapeless clothes were mismatched shades of brown. In her right hand, she held an old-fashioned medical bag.

"I'm Lucy Carrington. Ken said you needed a doctor?" Her cut-glass accent told her biography in a few syllables—homes in the poshest parts of London, expensive schooling, and a social network composed of one-percenters.

"We do need a doctor, but you won't be able to help him. The man's definitely dead." I needed to delay her, buy time for the guys to stash Jocelyn's stuff.

Lucy's response was interrupted by the heavy tread of footsteps.

Bernice's furry head appeared in the doorway of the other apartment in the same instant that a man crested the head of the stone staircase and stepped into the hall.

Thrilled by the prospect of a new playmate, Bernice engaged in an ecstasy of barking. She barreled through the crowd and leaped at the newcomer. The man was in his mid-fifties, with hair that looked as though someone had hacked it with a chainsaw. He side-stepped the dog and backed against the wall. She pinned him in place with her paws and subjected him to a thorough licking.

Seeing that no one else felt inclined to come to the man's rescue, I resigned myself to the inevitable.

"Get down, Bernice." I grabbed her collar and tugged gently.

I expected her to ignore me. Instead, the dog leaped at me and treated me to the same slobbery greeting she'd given the stranger. Once Bernice was satisfied that she'd licked every square centimeter of exposed skin, she dropped to all fours, wagged her tail, and went off in pursuit of new prey.

The man pulled a cloth handkerchief from his pocket and wiped his face. "You need to keep your dog under control," he growled at me in broken English.

I gave a wide-palmed shrug. "Not my dog, not my responsibility."

He glared at me beneath a pair of caterpillar eyebrows. I knew who—or rather, what—he was before he held up his ID card. "*Ispettore Capo* Colombo, State Police. We had a report of murder in this building."

Chief Inspector Colombo's rumpled beige raincoat, in addition to his name, left me stranded somewhere between a laugh and a panic attack. "A chief inspector is already on the doorstep? Impressive. The Italian police move fast."

Colombo swiped a finger as though he were operating a touchscreen device. The gesture was both dismissive and offensive, as I was sure he'd intended it to be. "Step aside, please. I need to view the body." His eyes swiveled from one apartment door to the other, then raked the crowd. "Which one of you called the police?"

Ken sprang forward, obsequious to a fault. "Me, sir. I'm Ken Heaton. My girlfriend and I live downstairs."

Colombo grunted. "Who found the body?"

I raised my hand. "I did."

Which was true. I had found the dead dude. No need to mention Sidney had found him first. There'd be plenty of time to discuss that detail when Colombo had examined the body.

The detective's years on the job had left his face frozen into an accusatory scowl. He turned the full force of his glare on me. "And you are?"

"Visiting my half-brother," I replied, whip-sharp and cheeky. I schooled my features into an innocent expression.

The scowl deepened. "I meant, what's your name?"

"My legal name is Angélique Doyle. I go by Kimmy." I didn't add that I'd adopted the moniker within the last couple of hours.

"Which apartment is the body in?"

89

The inspector addressed the question to me, but Ken inserted himself into the conversation once again. "It's in there." He pointed at Jocelyn's door. "The man who lives there is called Jocelyn Dingus-Cockett. He's a mystery writer. Now he has a dead body in his apartment. Ironic, isn't it?" Ken couldn't contain his smirk. "And it happened the very week he persuaded our landlord to get rid of the villa's surveillance cameras. I call that suspicious. Don't you?"

The look Colombo cast him could have curdled cream. "I'll decide what's suspicious. For now, I want all of you to wait in your apartments until an officer takes your statement. No one is to leave the building. Is that understood?"

A murmur of assent rippled through the crowd, but no one moved.

"That means now," the inspector growled. "No loitering."

With palpable reluctance, the onlookers trooped back into the party hosts' apartment. Dani shot me a meaningful look before grabbing Bernice's collar and urging the dog to follow. When the door closed behind them, only Lucy, Colombo, and I remained in the hallway.

My heart thumped against my ribs. Colombo's arrival had discombobulated me. When I'd asked Barbie and Ken to call the cops, I'd expected a couple of local uniforms to show up, not a plainclothes inspector. While Jocelyn's antics might have gone unnoticed by less experienced police officers, this man didn't miss a trick. He exuded the careworn weariness and jagged edges of a seasoned detective.

Colombo made to move to Jocelyn's door, but I neatly blocked his path. "Before you go inside, I'd like to see your ID close up. With a killer on the loose, I'm understandably wary of strangers."

I was stalling for time. Surely the guys had gotten rid of Jocelyn's research by now?

My request to examine his ID didn't go down well. A muscle in his cheek flexed. His entire body quivered with the pent-up aggression that police officers so often shared with the criminals they hunted. The inspector locked eyes with me, waging a silent battle he was destined to lose. I'd grown up surrounded by alpha males. I was used to standing my ground against men who were bigger, stronger, tougher than me. Besides, Colombo's little macho display played right into my hands. The more time I could give the guys to get rid of Jocelyn's research material, the better.

That time was regrettably short. With a fluid snap-flick of his wrist, Colombo held his ID card under my nose. "Here you go."

I took it gingerly between my thumb and forefinger, just as I'd handle a dangerous object. Then I squinted at the card, making a show of examining it from every angle. When I could no longer reasonably hold on to the ID, I returned it and gestured to Jocelyn's apartment. "Go on in."

Colombo stalked inside, bow-legged and belligerent, pausing in the entrance just long enough to don plastic slippers and latex gloves. I'd annoyed him and he'd hold it against me. Not an ideal situation, especially when the last thing I needed was a cop on my case, but it couldn't be helped.

I stayed where I was, ears cocked for any sign I needed to leg it. A rumble of male voices sounded from the living room, but I couldn't hear what they were saying. On the plus side, I wasn't getting a fight-or-flight vibe. I was so preoccupied with my attempt to eavesdrop that I'd totally forgotten about the doctor.

Lucy still hovered in the hallway, clutching her old-fashioned black medical bag, shifting her weight from one foot to the other. "Can I come in now?"

"Yes, of course." I stepped aside, ushering her into the apartment. "How's your Italian? If you're stuck, I can help with the lingo."

Relief flooded her round face, bringing a touch of color to her wan cheeks. "You speak Italian? Wonderful. I might need help with translating. That's assuming the police inspector wants me to stay." She grimaced. "I'm a pediatrician in private practice. Murders aren't in my usual line. However, I'll do my best to help."

"You might not need to. Colombo's bound to call in a forensic pathologist. I imagine they'll arrive any moment."

"Forensics won't get here for at least ninety

minutes." Lucy dropped her voice to a whisper, glancing nervously around as though the killer—or the chief inspector—might leap out from a concealed space to accost her. "Or so Ken said when he got off the phone from the emergency services. They're busy at a crime scene in Genoa. That's why Chief Inspector Colombo is here. He lives in this neighborhood."

"That explains his fast arrival on the scene." I stretched out a hand. "I'm Kimmy, by the way. I'm staying in apartment six with Dani."

"That makes us temporary neighbors." Lucy's handshake was firmer than I'd expected from her meek demeanor. "Nice to meet you. I wish it was under happier circumstances."

"Yeah, same. It's been quite an evening." I pointed to the living room. "The body's this way."

Lucy straightened her back. "Okay. I can do this."

I hesitated for a moment before following her. Should I stay? Or should I go across to talk to Dani? We had to address the ransom demand and figure out our next step in the search for Del. Yet I couldn't abandon Sidney with Colombo and Jocelyn. After all, I was the reason he'd come to Monterosso.

I sucked in air and steeled my shoulders. It was time to spin a web and hope I didn't tie myself up with my lies.

## 10

*B*ack in the living room, the cats hadn't budged from the sofa. However, their number had increased from four to six. Wide-eyed and alert, twelve eyes watched the inspector examine the body.

There was no sign of Sidney. I presumed he'd absconded with Jocelyn's laptop and research material, probably out the window that now stood ajar. A welcome breeze blew through the opening, lowering the room's temperature from boiling to merely stifling.

Jocelyn loitered by the kitchen bar, looking as shifty as a crook in a Christmas pantomime. Now that he'd shed his outdoor coat, I saw that he'd exchanged the red kimono he'd worn earlier for a slightly less bedraggled blue version. He still wore his battered leather sandals. His orange-tinted spectacles perched on the end of his nose. He regarded me over their gold rims, making absurd eye movements I guessed conveyed a wordless warning.

While Lucy introduced herself to the grumpy inspector, I perched on the arm of the armchair where I'd thrown my jacket. I'd expected Colombo to kick Jocelyn and me out the moment the doctor arrived, but he didn't seem to care about our presence. He was wholly absorbed in his scrutiny of the body. Although the forensics team was bound to take professional shots, Colombo snapped photos with his phone.

Why hadn't I thought to do that before fetching help? If my brother's disappearance was connected to the murder, having crime scene photos would help my investigation.

Lucy slipped on a pair of latex gloves and joined the inspector by the dead man. Careful not to disturb the body unduly, she carried out a preliminary medical examination. I'd encountered several murder victims in the past. However, I'd never had the opportunity to see how professionals approached a crime scene. I was interested in picking up tips for my future P.I. career— a career that might crash on takeoff if I didn't find my brother within the next twenty-four hours. My cunning plan to catch a flight to Florida tomorrow was looking less likely by the second.

While Colombo and Lucy did their thing, I soaked up every detail of the crime scene. I was better with facts than with people. In other circumstances, I'd have inspected the scene the instant I walked into the room

—sifting through the minutia, forming ideas. The dog's antics, followed by Sidney's unexpected presence, and then Jocelyn's unusual behavior, had distracted me from focusing on the murder victim. Now that I had the leisure to take in the body and its surroundings, several points struck me as odd.

First, the lack of blood. I'd encountered stabbing victims before, some as recently as this weekend. This man lay face down on what appeared to be a pristinely white sheepskin rug. The second strange point was the rug itself. Jocelyn's apartment was a generous size, with a lovely view. However, his furniture looked like relics from a dumpster dive, and his clothes were a cross between a political zealot and an escaped mental patient. The sheepskin rug was luxuriant and fluffy and totally out of place. And hadn't Jocelyn described it as awful? If he didn't like the rug, why was it in his apartment?

The third odd point was the blood on Sidney. It had appeared sticky, not runny. That told me the man had been dead for a while. The space around the body was a blood-free zone. How had Sidney wound up with blood on his hands? From checking the guy for a pulse? Was there blood beneath the body?

"The heat of the fire makes it difficult to be precise," Lucy said in halting Italian that was far more fluent than she'd led me to believe. "I estimate death occurred at least twelve hours ago. Possibly as long as sixteen."

Colombo checked his wristwatch. "It's nineteen-hundred now. That puts time of death at between three and seven in the morning."

She nodded. "That's my best guess. Perhaps the pathologist can narrow it down for you."

My insides turned to liquid nitrogen. Marco had last seen my brother at between six and six-thirty, and Dani had said it was a half-hour walk from Marco's place to the villa. Del's kidnapping had to be connected to the murder. But how?

"The absence of blood around the body is strange." Lucy's thin lips twisted and relaxed in a nervous rinse-repeat. "I don't think he was killed here."

"He wasn't killed on this rug," Colombo clarified. "He might have been stabbed on the floor and placed on the rug after death."

"And the blood?" The words were out of my mouth before I could stop myself. "If the man was killed in this room, surely the floor would have been covered in the stuff."

Colombo regarded me through emotionless hazel eyes. "The killer could have cleaned the floor."

"And positioned the body on the rug once it had stopped bleeding? Why? As some sort of trophy?"

"Impossible." Jocelyn bristled with equal measures of panic and indignation. "I was here the whole day. If that man died in the early hours of the morning, he wasn't killed in my apartment. And the rug? I've never seen it before."

I couldn't decide if Sidney's cousin's precise Italian or his earlobe sweat fascinated me more. Before I'd had time to ponder the matter further, the police inspector pounced on Jocelyn's statement. "This isn't your rug? Are you sure?"

Jocelyn regarded Colombo over the rims of his colorful spectacles. "I'm vegan, inspector. That's a sheepskin rug."

Colombo took in Jocelyn's footwear. "You're wearing leather sandals."

"*Vegan* leather. I don't eat or wear animals."

The police inspector allowed several uncomfortable seconds to pass while we watched him mentally summing up the scene of the crime. Lucy remained absolutely silent, as though hoping the inspector would forget she was there and therefore forget to send her packing. She wanted to hear what the inspector would ask next, as did I.

He didn't leave us hanging for long.

Colombo came out of his trance with a start and rounded on Jocelyn. "If Ms. Doyle found the body, where were you at the time?"

"At the party across the hall. I was there from six-fifteen until I went down to the basement with one of the other guests to get supplies. When we got back upstairs, I heard the dog barking. I don't know how the beast got into my apartment, but she did. When I walked in, I found Kimmy and the dog in my living room, standing over the dead body."

No mention of Sidney. I wondered what agreement the men had come to while I was holding back the tide outside.

"I'd taken Bernice for a walk," I supplied before the inspector could ask. "When we got back to the villa, Jocelyn and Barbie let us into the courtyard."

"Barbie?" The inspector snapped the question.

"Barbie Drake," Jocelyn supplied. "The neighbor who helped me get supplies from the basement. She lives with Ken Heaton in apartment three. Lovely girl. No idea what she sees in that twat."

Colombo didn't respond to this swipe against Ken's character, but something that might have been amusement flickered in his eyes. Jocelyn disliked Ken. Colombo would file that nugget of information away for future reference. "What do Ms. Drake and Mr. Heaton do?"

"She's an out-of-work actress who works shifts at a gelateria in town. He's employed by a tech company in Milan, but works from home four days a week." Jocelyn scowled. "Worst luck. I encounter him far too often for my taste."

Colombo tapped the nib of his pen against his notebook. "Who else lives at Villa Margherita?"

"Saul and Riccardo Ventimiglia are photographers who run a photography studio in Monterosso. They're the ones hosting tonight's party. Maria Bianchi lives in apartment four. She's a retired civil servant. Widowed, I believe. Dani and Jimmy O'Brien live in apartment six. She's heavily pregnant. His occupation is a mystery." Jocelyn looked pointedly at me. "Jimmy is Kimmy's brother."

"That leaves apartment five," Colombo said. "Who lives there?"

Lucy raised a tentative hand. "I'm staying there for a week with my sister, Heather."

"A weekly rental," Jocelyn supplied, anticipating Colombo's next question. "Tourists or people visiting family."

Colombo scribbled something in his notebook before turning back to me. "What happened after Ms. Heaton and Mr. Dingus-Cockett let you into the property? What did you do next?"

"Barbie told me my brother's girlfriend was upstairs at the villa residents' weekly potluck party. She suggested I go up and join them."

"So you came up to this floor. Where was the dog?"

"Bernice was with me. Apparently, tonight's hosts don't mind a large dog in their apartment."

"But she's not welcome in mine," Jocelyn snapped. "That dog must have added lockpicking skills to her evil repertoire. I locked the door before I went across the hall. The key's still in my pocket."

I jerked around. "Your door was open when Bernice and I reached this floor. I don't know if it was the scent of the cats, the corpse, or the opportunity to explore forbidden territory, but she hotpawed in here at warp speed."

"That's impossible," Jocelyn huffed. "It was closed when Barbie and I went downstairs, and that was two, three minutes before you and Bernice came up here."

Colombo eyed us both for a lead-loaded moment. "I want you two to look at the body."

"It's hard to look at anything else," Jocelyn quipped. "I'll have nightmares about those naked buttocks."

For the first time since we'd met, the suspicion of a smile threatened to break through the inspector's grim expression. "I want you to look at his *face*, not his behind. Dr. Carrington, can you help me lift his head?"

Lucy helped Colombo angle the dead man's head so that his face was visible. He was older than the jet-black hair had led me to believe and had to be in his early sixties or even older. His blue lips, and blank, staring eyes were the stuff of horror movies.

I wrapped my arms around myself. "I've never seen him before."

Jocelyn's strangled intake of breath drew all our attention. Whey-faced, he slumped onto the sofa, eliciting a yowl of protest from the cat he'd just used as a cushion. "Good grief. It's Lucky."

"Lucky?" My question was as much in response to the hilariously stereotypical mobster name as it was a request for more information. "Given the circumstances, Lucky's name is even more of a misnomer than my own."

"I need his full name and address," Colombo barked.

"Don't you recognize him, Inspector? He's a local celebrity—at least, according to himself." Jocelyn glanced at the body, and a spasm of revulsion crossed his face. "This is Lucky Lucchese. His Monterosso address is here. This is Lucky's apartment."

The inspector betrayed not a flicker of surprise. "Lucky is your lover?"

The notion of a relationship with Lucky appeared to entertain Jocelyn. "Lucky is a pain in his skinny white buttocks. Ours was a business relationship. No more, no less."

Colombo's gaze sharpened. "What sort of business relationship?"

"Get your mind out of the gutter, inspector. I met Lucky at a writers' conference in L.A. several years ago."

My ears pricked up, and my eyes dropped to the dead guy. "Wait a sec. Is this Lucky Lucchese the American mystery author? The one who recently signed a mega deal with the Crimeflix streaming service?"

"Yeah," Jocelyn replied. "Lucky writes mobster mysteries, mostly set in the US, but he also has a series set in Italy. He lives in Monterosso for a few months each summer to research his Italian-set books. He was looking for a fellow writer to sublet this apartment for the months he's back in the US. I was looking for a place to spend the winter that wasn't England. This is my second winter in Italy. It was the perfect arrangement."

"Perfect until one of you ended up murdered." Colombo eased Lucky back into the position he'd been in when I'd found him. "This potluck dinner—what time did it begin?"

"Six o'clock, but I didn't get there until a quarter past. The weekly dinners are buffet-style and drop in, drop out. People come and go as they please."

"Where were you before you went to your neighbor's apartment?"

"Holed up in here, working on my book. Trust me, I'd have noticed a corpse cluttering up my living room, especially one with a poker in its back."

Colombo drew his bushy brows together. "Are you sure you didn't leave your apartment before the party?"

Jocelyn turned an accusatory glare on me. "Only to let *her* in. Must've been around five this evening. But I was back here within ten minutes, max, and no one dumped a body on me while I was gone."

"I'd arrived at the villa for the first time," I said, anticipating Colombo's next question. "I rang Jocelyn's bell by mistake. I wanted my brother's apartment, but I wasn't sure if he lived in one or six."

"When I got back after letting her in, I was alone. I'm telling you, someone snuck that body in here while I was across the hall at the party," Jocelyn insisted. "It's the only logical conclusion."

"I can think of several logical conclusions pertaining to this crime." Colombo's smile had a lupine quality. "Mr. Heaton says you write detective fiction. Perhaps you made your fantasies a reality—especially now you persuaded the landlord to get rid of the villa's security cameras."

Jocelyn snorted. "Ken Heaton is a snake. He loves to gossip, and he's not fussy about accuracy."

"What part of his story is untrue?"

"For a start, my specialty is investigative journalism, not fiction. I reveal the secrets our governments want concealed."

The inspector took this pompous pronouncement in his stride. "Is the dead man connected to a secret our governments want to hush up? How else do you think he wound up naked and dead in your apartment?"

"How should I know? I walked in here to rescue my cats from a rabid canine and found Kimmy hovering over the body."

I shot him a laser-hot glare. I'd helped this man conceal potential evidence from the police. And how did he repay me? By throwing me under the proverbial bus.

"You haven't answered my question about the surveillance cameras," Colombo said, his tone arch.

"I wasn't aware you'd asked one," Jocelyn shot back. "You made a statement about me persuading the landlord to remove the villa's security cameras. That's not true. I'm passionate about privacy. The villa has an alarm system. There's no need to film our comings and goings in the name of safety."

"Did you ask the villa's owner to remove the cameras?"

"No. I asked him to provide the residents with information about exactly what was being recorded and for a guarantee that any footage would be deleted after seventy-two hours. He responded by switching off the entire system."

Colombo's gaze swiveled to Lucy before Jocelyn responded. "What can you tell me about the contention over the surveillance cameras?"

Lucy removed her latex gloves and returned her equipment to her medical bag. "Absolutely nothing. I'm only here for a week, remember?"

"And yet you were invited to a party hosted by the couple in apartment two?" Colombo's bushy eyebrows formed twin V-s of skepticism. "Are they friends of yours?"

"The Sunday evening potluck dinners are a villa tradition," Jocelyn interjected. "The residents of apartments two, three, four, and six take turns hosting. We all contribute food and drink. In my case, wine—I don't cook. Everyone's invited, including whoever's renting the holiday apartment."

"Do you never act as host to one of these parties?" I asked, beating Colombo to the punch.

Jocelyn's lip curled. "As I said, I value my privacy. I

don't allow people in my apartment. Today's contingent is a positive invasion."

A loud rap sounded on the door. "Police," called a man's voice. "Open up."

Colombo swaggered to the door and let in two uniformed policemen. "Are there only two of you? I asked for at least four officers."

"We split up, sir. Perotta and Abate are guarding the entrance."

The inspector grunted. "I need one of you to drive Ms. Doyle and Mr. Dingus-Cockett to the station. Meanwhile, the other can question everyone at the villa and arrange for them to come to the station tomorrow to sign their statements."

Now that I was officially the first person on the scene of the crime, it wasn't surprising that Colombo was insisting on hauling me to the police station. But it was dashed inconvenient. I needed to be free to look for my brother. Plus, I had no clue where Sidney was, and no idea what he'd learned from Jocelyn.

"I can't leave my brother's girlfriend," I said. "She's pregnant. She could go into labor at any moment."

Colombo's hard stare pinned me in place. "If she does, we'll bring her to the hospital. And if you really want to be there to hold her hand, the sooner you give your statement, the better."

## 11

*C*hief Inspector Colombo kept me at the police station until the early hours of Monday morning. I can sum the experience up in two words: tedious and frustrating. This wasn't my first rodeo at a cop shop. I'd "helped the police with their inquiries" in the past. However, being questioned for murder was a novel experience and not one I enjoyed. Unlike the tensely dramatic interrogation scenes I'd watched on TV, the reality comprised repeated questions, paperwork, a half-hour snooze in an uncomfortable cell, and my bored lawyer's constant refrain of, "You don't need to answer that question."

It had taken all my ingenuity to explain my visit to Monterosso and my relationship with Del without revealing my brother's legal name. I had no choice but to tell mine. The police's first demand was to see my ID—understandable, but a nuisance. When I told

Colombo that my brother and I were half-siblings, I let him and his subordinates assume we had different surnames. I knew I had to get ahead of the ridiculous story I'd told Barbie about Del and I being twins named Jimmy and Kimmy, so I told the cops we were born three months apart (true), and he'd nicknamed me Kimmy (untrue).

At four-thirty in the morning, Colombo's bleary-eyed sidekick let me leave on the condition I surrendered my passport or national ID card and agreed to remain in the area. I handed over my French national ID card, conveniently forgetting to mention my Irish passport, which was still in the boot of the rental car. Technically, I wasn't supposed to travel with both documents, but I'd lived life on the gray side of the law for long enough to know how to use my status as a dual national to my advantage.

My lawyer was a disheveled fifty-something named Alberto Alessi. Alberto's was the first name I'd found when I'd searched for a local lawyer to represent me. He had the dejected air of a man who had low expectations of life and found that life lived down to them.

As we left the interrogation room, he handed me a grease-stained business card. "Not a word to the cops without me present," he muttered under his garlic-fumed breath. "They don't trust you, and *I* don't trust you not to get snarky with them."

I revised my opinion of Alberto's incompetence.

He might look like he slept in his suit, but he had a knack for reading people. Under the circumstances, this realization weighed uncomfortably on my tired shoulders. The last thing I needed was this lawyer figuring out my real reason for being in Monterosso.

I pocketed the card. "Thanks, Alberto. I'll be in touch."

Alberto and I parted ways in the police station's cramped lobby. I hadn't seen Jocelyn since we'd arrived at the station, and there was no sign of him now. I doubted the police had let him go home. The questions Colombo and Co. had asked me clarified Jocelyn was their prime suspect, and I was a mere Also Ran.

Were they correct? Jocelyn and Lucky had shared an apartment, albeit at different times. And both men wrote about crime. Was there a connection between Lucky's work and his murder? If so, could it be connected to the research material Jocelyn was so eager to conceal from the police?

The police officer in charge at the front desk was the same grandmotherly woman who'd checked in Jocelyn and me when we'd arrived. She'd already piled my jacket, phone, and backpack on the counter.

She beamed when I approached the desk, clearly unfazed by my status as a murder suspect. "Hello, dear. You must be exhausted."

"I can barely stand. I need a shower and a bed, and not necessarily in that order."

She inclined her head in a kindly nod. "I

understand. Before you go, please check your belongings and then sign this form to confirm they're all present and correct. I've printed a receipt for your ID card. You can collect it when Chief Inspector Colombo is further along in his inquiries."

"In other words, when he's finally struck me off the suspect list." I kept my tone light, but the ID business worried me. In theory, I could try to leave Italy using my Irish passport, but skipping town during a murder investigation would land me in the soup, regardless of my innocence. I wanted to become a licensed P.I. for an international private investigation agency. Because of the Omega Group's proximity to the Italian border, we had a lot of cases in Italy. Getting on the wrong side of the Italian police before I even had my license would be a foolish move.

I opened my backpack and made sure everything was there. Then I pulled on my jacket and pocketed the receipt for my ID. "Where do I need to sign?"

The police officer handed me an itemized list, and I scrawled my signature at the bottom.

When I gave it back it to her, she slid a keycard across the desk. "Your friend Sidney dropped in and left you a message. He's staying at L'Hotel del Gigante. Room 122. This keycard will also open the front door."

A wave of relief spilled over me. Whether the prospect of spilling all to Sidney enticed me more than the promise of a bed, I couldn't say, but the idea of both brought me joy. "Where is L'Hotel del Gigante?"

The woman inclined her head to the left. "Five doors down this street. The sign above the door is missing the G. You can't miss it."

I slid the keycard into my pocket. "Thanks. Have a good night."

Outside the police station, I switched on my phone. It immediately pinged with two messages. Both were from Dani.

The first ran as follows:

*"The kidnappers contacted me. They want the twenty-five thousand in unmarked notes by ten p.m. tomorrow. They'll be in touch to arrange a drop-off point. Please call me as soon as you can."*

The second message reiterated our need to talk and invited me to meet Dani for breakfast at the villa if the police released me in time, or brunch, if that suited me better. She'd had no more updates from Del's kidnappers regarding the ransom.

I shoved my phone back in my pocket and felt the rumblings of a headache. How could I get my paws on twenty-five grand? Could Dani? Would her relatives help her out? I had to hope so because I didn't have that kind of money lying around, and I had no idea how to amass such a sum by legal means.

I was still mulling over this dilemma when I reached Sidney's hotel. L'Hotel del Gigante inhabited a narrow, three-storied building. Under the glow of the streetlights, the facade appeared orange, but it was probably closer to yellow in natural light.

I slid the keycard into the lock and stepped into a dimly lit foyer. The reception was unoccupied. A sign next to a buzzer invited late-night visitors to press if they needed help. I crept up the creaking staircase and found room 122.

To give Sidney a heads-up that his room was about to be invaded, I rapped on the door five times—two long, three short—the code we'd used during our Alpine adventure.

A crash sounded in the room, followed by muffled swearing. The next moment, Sidney wrenched open the door before I'd inserted the keycard. He was fully dressed, right down to his designer sneakers. His expression was haggard, and he looked as exhausted as I felt.

While I surveyed him, he returned the favor. "Angel, you look like roadkill."

"I feel like roadkill. I haven't had a decent night's sleep since... when did we leave Nice? Early Friday morning? Then the night of Wednesday to Thursday."

I shuffled into Sidney's room and looked around. The room was the dictionary definition of poky. Two twin beds of unequal height had been shoved together to form a lopsided whole. A wardrobe and chest of drawers took up the rest of the space, forcing me to sidle past them to reach the unoccupied side of the bed.

I pulled off my jacket and boots and collapsed onto the mattress. Any motivation to shower had evaporated, especially as I suspected the bathroom was designed on similarly elbow-bashing proportions. Also, I was too tired to think straight, let alone figure out which knicker leg was which.

Sidney removed his sneakers and lay on his mattress. "Is Jocelyn still at the police station?"

"I think so." I stifled a yawn. "The way the cops were grilling me, I got the impression that Jocelyn is their prime suspect."

"Good news for you, bad news for Jocelyn."

He sounded morose, piquing my curiosity.

"I didn't get the impression you two were close," I said. "Or did I misread your interaction?"

"We're not close, but Jocelyn's not a bad bloke. Weird and annoying, but not violent. In the unlikely event he killed someone, I can't imagine him stabbing a man with a poker. Jocelyn's more squeamish about blood than I am."

"If Jocelyn didn't kill Lucky, then who did? Your cousin was mighty cagey about his book research."

"Jocelyn's default setting is paranoid. He's the quintessential conspiracy theorist. He always thinks government spies are on his tail."

I rolled onto my side and fluffed up my pillows. "Why does he hate the police? I'm not a fan, but I have my reasons. What are his?"

Sidney lay on his back and stared at the damp-stained ceiling. "Jocelyn's father—my great uncle Mortimer was a high court judge. He was renowned in his field, and famous for putting away several high-profile criminals. When Jocelyn was a kid, his father was a passerby during a bank robbery."

"I'm sensing this story doesn't have a happy ending. What happened to Jocelyn's dad?"

"The robbery devolved into a shootout between the police and the robbers. Mortimer was fatally wounded in the crossfire. After the postmortem, it transpired that the bullet that killed him came from a police weapon. Just one of those horrendous wrong place, wrong time scenarios. Unfortunately, Jocelyn became convinced that his father's death was part of a conspiracy connected to his work at the high court. That triggered my cousin's lifelong obsession with conspiracy theories."

"How awful. Could Jocelyn be right? Was there a link between his father's work and the bank robbery?"

"There was an inquiry, and it concluded that Mortimer's death was simply a tragic accident. Jocelyn's grief turned into an unhealthy fixation." Sidney rolled onto his side and propped himself up on his elbow. "But enough about my cousin. Why did you come to Monterosso, Angel? I've pieced some of it together from what Jocelyn said, but I'm missing chunks of info."

I buried my face into my pillow and groaned. "It's a classic case of 'no good deed goes unpunished.' I wish

I'd ignored my inner nice girl and caught that plane to Florida."

"Jocelyn says your brother lives in one of the villa's apartments. I didn't know you had a brother called Jimmy."

"That's because I don't. Jimmy is the name Del's using in Italy. He left London under a cloud and is effectively hiding out."

"And the pregnant girl at the villa is his partner?" Sidney asked.

"Apparently. I hadn't met her until today." I checked my watch. "Make that yesterday."

Sidney digested this for a moment. "So the text message you got in the car on the way to the airport was from Del's girlfriend?"

"No, it was from Del." I found the messages on my phone and handed Sidney the device. "Here you go."

He scanned the screen, the frown line between his brows deepening. "What sort of trouble is he in?"

"The sort that costs twenty-five thousand euros to get out of." In a few succinct sentences, I filled Sidney in on the Luigi Genero connection and the ransom demand.

When I'd finished, he let out a low whistle. "And I thought you were a trouble magnet. Sounds like your brother has you beat. Do you think Anna-Sofia—or Dani—is telling the truth?"

I scrunched my nose. "I'm not sure. I don't entirely

trust her. That said, she's scared, and I don't think she's faking her fear."

"I'd be scared if I was hiding out from a psycho mobster," Sidney mused, tapping a finger against his chin. "Why don't you think this Genero character is behind Del's kidnapping?"

"Because Luigi supposedly wants to find Dani and Del and punish them for running away together. In Luigi's world, punish is synonymous with kill. Why would he waste time kidnapping my brother and demanding a ludicrously low ransom for his safe return?"

"I don't consider twenty-five thousand euros a ludicrously low amount," Sidney said. "Particularly not in my financially precarious state."

"Nor do I, but Luigi Genero is loaded. Twenty-five grand is nothing to him."

"But it is to Del and Dani, especially with a baby on the way," Sidney pointed out. "Perhaps Luigi wants to toy with them before he has them killed. Look, I'm not saying you're wrong to suspect someone else is behind the kidnapping, but I wouldn't strike Luigi off the suspect list just yet."

"Fair enough. Luigi stays on the list." A yawn escaped me, prompting him to yawn in sympathy. "Sorry, Sidney. My eyelids have weights pulling them down. And I haven't even asked you about Jocelyn's infamous research material."

"You can ask me after we've had some sleep. What time does Dani expect you at her apartment?"

"She didn't specify." I tapped out a message and hit send. "I've suggested I swing by at ten. That gives me time to sleep and shower."

"And time for us to come up with a plan."

I frowned at him. "There's no 'us,' Sidney. You need to book a flight to Florida. Why should you jeopardize your P.I. career?"

"For the same reason you hightailed it to Italy." He waved a hand when I objected. "I'm serious, Angel. I need to stay to help Jocelyn, and you need to stay to help Del. Between us, we can get to the bottom of whatever's going on in Monterosso."

I wasn't so optimistic, but the news that Sidney was staying came as an immense relief. In different circumstances, I'd have been excited we were embarking on two new investigations. I just wished one didn't involve my idiot brother.

12

Three hours of uninterrupted sleep later, I
hauled my still-tired carcass up the hill to
Villa Margherita. Sidney and I had parted company
outside the police station. He wanted to check on
Jocelyn and see what he could discover about the
murder investigation. We'd arranged to meet in the
afternoon, the time to be specified once I knew more
about the ransom demand and how that affected my
search for Del.

Before leaving the hotel, I'd sent my mother a text
message, appraising her of the situation. She'd read
the text seconds after I'd hit send but hadn't
responded. I sensed waves of fury rolling across the
Mediterranean Sea from Nice to Monterosso. I
couldn't blame her for being angry. She'd taken a
chance on Sidney and me and offered us the career
opportunity of our dreams. And now I'd blown it by

running to Del's rescue and becoming embroiled in a murder investigation.

The weather was warmer than yesterday. Halfway up the incline to the villa, my back was slick with sweat. I shed my jacket and stretched my sore limbs. My leg muscles ached after yesterday's walk-run with Bernice. My head was no less painful. I'd hoped that sleep and a shower would bring clarity to my jumbled thoughts. Instead, I'd woken with a headache and more questions than answers.

Why had Del reached out to me for help? Why not Dad or one of our brothers? Surely they were better placed than me to advise Del on dealing with the Genero gang? Our father had cut ties with me because I'd informed on his boss's son, but there was no reason to suppose he'd done the same to Del. Unless things had changed over the last year, the crooks my father associated with were too small-fry to bother the Generos. Or had Luigi extended his wrath to my father when Del did a bunk with his wife?

By the time I reached the villa, I was no closer to finding answers, and my stubbornly silent phone burned an invisible hole in my pocket. A police car was parked outside the villa, and the gates were open a crack. Somewhere within, a dog howled. After a furtive glance from side to side, I slipped into the courtyard and crash-banged into Chief Inspector Colombo.

We reeled back and locked eyes.

"Ms. Doyle." His curled-lipped greeting combined

disdain with suspicion. My only consolation was that he looked as rough as I felt.

Bernice's persistent howling wasn't helping my headache, but I forced a saccharine smile. "Good morning, Inspector. Found the killer yet?"

A muscle in his cheek flexed. "Do you have anything to add to your statement? News of your brother's whereabouts, perhaps?"

His mention of Del spiked my already soaring stress levels. "Why are you so interested in my brother? He wasn't here last night."

"Precisely. And no one seems to know when he'll be back, least of all his girlfriend." The man took a step closer—close enough for me to smell the espresso on his breath. "Funny time for you to come to Monterosso. Why didn't you plan your visit for when your brother was here?"

"I don't know if you noticed, but his girlfriend is about to pop. And she's not having an easy pregnancy. They asked me to stay with her while Jimmy's away." This was a reiteration of the story I'd told during my hours of questioning.

Colombo's expression developed a predatory gleam. "Yet Jimmy's girlfriend claims she didn't know you were coming to visit. Doesn't that strike you as strange?"

*Blast.* Dani and I hadn't had an opportunity to prep our respective stories. I'd had to wing mine and hope she didn't contradict me. Unfortunately, it seemed that she had.

"My brother asked me to come and stay with Dani, but she didn't want company. What can I say? It's awkward. I'm staying at a hotel and checking in with her regularly."

"Staying with the friend who dropped off the keycard at the station?"

Colombo tossed the question at me like a grenade, but I'd been prepared for it. I'd expected the police officer at the front desk to tell him about Sidney's visit.

"That's right." I tossed a question right back at him. "Did any of the villa residents see Lucky arrive yesterday?"

The man scowled. "They say not, but I'm not so sure."

"Did you find his clothes? Surely he didn't show up to the villa wearing nothing but his birthday suit?"

"I doubt he strolled through Monterosso naked," he replied dryly. "But, no, we haven't found his clothes—yet. They can't have disappeared into thin air."

I nodded toward Dani's door, where Bernice strained against her leash. "I need to go now before the dog injures herself, trying to get to me."

Colombo's stony gaze bore into me. "One last question."

"My lawyer advised me not to talk to you without his presence," I said sweetly. "This conversation is over."

I tried to move past him, but he blocked my path. "I indulged your curiosity, Ms. Doyle. It's time for you to return the favor. Do you read crime fiction?"

"Who doesn't?" The question was so unexpected that I answered it without thinking.

"Have you read any of Lucky Lucchese's mysteries?"

"No. I'm not fond of mobster books." Where was he going with these questions? Was he implying I might be a crazed fan?

"Is there a problem, Kimmy? Do you need me to call your lawyer?" Dani appeared in the doorway of her apartment, ignoring Bernice's plaintive whines to be let back inside.

The chief inspector's hard eyes swiveled toward Dani. "What about you, *signora*?" he called. "Have you read any of Lucky Lucchese's books?"

Dani stared at him, expressionless. "I've read a couple. They make decent beach reads."

"What about Jocelyn Dingus-Cockett?" Colombo continued, switching back to English and addressing me. "Have you read any of his books?"

"What do our reading preferences have to do with the murder?" I asked, partly out of frustration, partly out of curiosity. "Is there a connection between the murder method and one of Lucky's books?"

A flash of fury zapped across Colombo's face. "I'm the one asking the questions. Just answer me."

I folded my arms across my chest. "This sounds

suspiciously like another interrogation. If you want to talk to me, let's do it at the station—with my lawyer present."

He glared at me, but this time, he stood aside and let me pass. I felt his intense stare drilling holes in my back as I crossed the courtyard to join Dani and Bernice.

The dog greeted me in an ecstasy of barking, tail-wagging, and peeing. Once Bernice had emptied her bladder, I leaned down to rub her furry head. "Why are you outside making such a racket?"

"Because Jocelyn's cats are inside." Dani rolled her eyes. "Yeah, I've been landed with them until Jocelyn gets home."

"Why did the heavily pregnant neighbor wind up with the cats? Couldn't one of the others take them in?"

"Ken claims he's allergic, and everyone else works outside the home. No one wants to look after six cats. If we could feed them in their own home, it'd be one thing, but Jocelyn's apartment is still a crime scene. At least Riccardo has agreed to deal with the kitty litter—I'm not supposed to touch it in my condition." Dani turned pleading dark eyes on me. "I don't suppose you could look after Bernice for a day or two? I can't walk her in my condition, and keeping her under the same roof as the cats isn't possible."

"I'm currently staying at a hotel. I don't know if they allow dogs."

"You could ask. Or you could stay with me and keep Bernice in the living room with you while I keep the cats in my bedroom."

I regarded the small living room with its three armchairs and no sofa. "Where am I supposed to sleep?"

"An armchair?" She flushed. "I'm sorry, but we only have one bed."

"In that case, I'd prefer to stay at the hotel."

"You could ask the management about Bernice," Dani insisted. "Many hotels here allow dogs for a small fee."

"Even if the hotel allows dogs, how do you expect me to look after Bernice while I'm trailing all over town looking for Del?" I caught her warning look and ground my teeth. "Fine. While I'm looking for *Jimmy*?"

Darting a glance at Chief Inspector Colombo, who was still glowering at us from the other side of the courtyard, Dani yanked my arm and pulled me into the apartment. Bernice tried to break free and join us, but Dani slammed the door on her. The dog's mournful howl was pitiful. I wasn't even a dog person, yet I wanted to give Bernice a reassuring cuddle.

"See what I mean?" Dani said as she led me up the steps to the kitchen. "It's not fair to leave the dog outside all day."

"I fail to see how this is my problem. I'm Del's sister, not your unpaid dogsitter."

Irritation flickered across Dani's face as she

lowered herself onto a chair at the kitchen table. "Jimmy. You're supposed to call him Jimmy."

"The only thing I'm supposed to be doing is a P.I. boot camp in Florida. Instead, here I am, dealing with my idiot brother's latest fiasco."

"I'm sorry if we've disrupted your plans," Dani drawled, not looking the least apologetic. "What do you expect me to do? I can't go out and look for him. Not in—"

"Your condition," I finished for her. "So you've said."

Jocelyn's Persian and ginger tabby made a meowing beeline for me, rubbing themselves against my legs and demanding my attention. I took the seat opposite Dani and let the ginger tabby sit on my lap. Not to be outdone by her sister, the Persian leaped onto the chair beside me and allowed me to pet her.

Dani wore a sulky expression. She snatched a slice of toast from the rack and tore it into pieces. "Are you implying I'm lying about not feeling well? Do you have any idea what it's like to be nine months pregnant? And now that silly man has gone and gotten himself killed."

"I didn't say you were lying." I helped myself to a cup of coffee from the espresso pot and placed a chocolate croissant on my plate. "Look, I don't want to argue with you. We're both on edge and worried about my brother. But however rotten you feel, I'm not your servant. I'll help the best I can, but don't boss me around."

By now, she'd completely shredded her uneaten toast and started destroying a second slice. "I'm sorry for being cranky. I hate feeling this helpless. The police were here first thing, asking more questions. I don't know what they think I can tell them. I barely knew Lucky."

"Didn't he attend the weekly potlucks?"

She screwed up her nose in thought. "Once. Maybe twice. Lucky usually dined out. Actually, he was hardly ever at the villa. I think he used it more as a crashpad than a home."

"Did the police search your apartment? Or anyone else's?"

Twin frown lines sprang up between Dani's perfectly styled brows. "No. Why would they?"

"Because Lucky wasn't killed in Jocelyn's living room. It's possible he died elsewhere in the building."

She shuddered and huddled inside her oversized cardigan. "Oh, I know all about that. The police found traces of blood in the basement. They think Lucky died there."

"Interesting," I mused. "Did they find anything else? Any clues to link Jocelyn to the crime?"

"I don't think so. Riccardo threw a fit about someone ransacking his costume collection. Apparently, he stores a few boxes in the basement, including one filled with carnival tat. Annoying for

Riccardo, but I can't see that having anything to do with the murder." She moved restlessly in her chair. "This is driving me crazy. I want to be out looking for Jimmy, especially seeing as it's my fault he's in this mess."

"Are you referring to Luigi? My brother knew the risk he was taking when he ran away with you." I took a bite of my chocolate croissant and almost swooned with delight. I hadn't eaten in over twenty-four hours, and I was famished.

Dani's dark eyes were sunken in their sockets, and her face was taut with strain. "The situation is more complicated than you realize. The kidnappers sent another note."

The chocolate croissant turned to sawdust on my tongue. I forced it down with a swig of espresso. "What does the new note say?"

"Nothing good." She removed a crumpled envelope from her cardigan pocket and slid it across the table to me.

I reached for it, then stopped myself. "Do you have gloves? Preferably of the disposable latex variety?"

She waved a hand in the kitchen's direction. "Second drawer to the left of the stove."

After dislodging the outraged ginger cat from my lap, I found a box of gloves and took two. Back at the table, I picked up the envelope and eased out the note. The sender had composed the message using crude cutout letters from a magazine.

*If you want to see your boyfriend alive, it'll cost you fifty-thousand euros. Deliver the money in unmarked fifty-euro banknotes by ten tomorrow night. The drop-off point will be confirmed an hour before the deadline.*

Dani stared at the note in disbelief. "Twenty-five thousand was bad enough. Where are we supposed to find fifty-thousand euros in cash?"

My stomach roiled, making me regret the chocolate croissant. "Doubling their demand is quite a leap. If they wanted fifty K, why not ask for it yesterday?"

"I don't know." Dani shoved her chair back from the table and stood. A tremor ran through her body, and she clasped her hands to stop them from shaking. "This can't be happening. We're supposed to be planning for the birth of our baby. Jimmy hasn't even finished setting up the crib."

I'd been wary of Dani yesterday, unsure how to read her. Today, there was no doubting the authenticity of her distress. "Do you have any idea where the kidnappers might keep him captive? When he texted me, he wanted us to meet at a place similar to our childhood hideout. That made me think of a tumbledown house or shed."

"The hills around Cinque Terre are littered with abandoned houses. Take any of the hiking trails, and you'll see several."

"That's what Barbie told me. Apart from the hills,

can you think of anywhere else a kidnapper might keep a captive?"

Dani paced the kitchen, her brow furrowed in thought. "A boat is another possibility. There are many inlets along the coast. The coast guard patrols regularly, but if the kidnappers are using a fishing boat, and they've intimidated Jimmy into keeping silent, the coast guard would have no reason to suspect foul play even if they searched the boat."

I downed the rest of my espresso and stood. "I'm going to talk to Marco again. And track down the elusive Alessandro. Maybe they'll be more forthcoming with information if I tell them my brother is in danger."

"What about the cash?" She chewed on her lower lip. "Do you think your father could help?"

I assessed her coolly, the old wariness back in force. "Dad doesn't have that kind of money. He's better at spending than saving."

"But he might have something to contribute. Like twenty thousand?"

"What about your uncle? If he's wealthy enough to own this villa, perhaps he has fifty thousand lying around."

"He doesn't have many liquid assets. I doubt he can get his hands on the cash by tomorrow."

I quirked an eyebrow. "If you expect me to call my father, a man I haven't spoken to in over two years, you'd better be prepared to go groveling to your relatives."

"It's not as if I have a choice," she said bitterly. "What happens if the kidnappers double the amount again?"

This thought had occurred to me. If they upped their demand a second time, I'd have to rethink my stance on not telling the police. "We'll deal with that scenario when and if it happens. For now, get busy on the phone while I track down Del's mates. For today, you concentrate on sourcing the cash, while I look for my brother. If the kidnappers get in touch with you again, send me a message. Otherwise, I'll contact you this evening."

"What about Bernice? Will you not consider bringing her with you?" Dani's tone was plaintive, her expression the perfect mix of hope and despair.

Aware I was being played for a fool, I regarded her warily. "Bernice is a big dog. She'll get in the way."

"She'll keep you safe, especially if you take the hiking trails. They'll be deserted at this time of year."

"Bernice loves everybody. She's more likely to play with the kidnappers than defend me."

Dani's long sigh was programmed to elicit sympathy. "I know you think I'm asking too much of you, but I really don't know what to do with the dog. She needs at least two long walks a day, and she's too boisterous to keep cooped up in the apartment, even without the cats to consider."

As if on cue, Bernice began howling again, the

noise slicing through my sore head and piercing my resolve.

"Fine," I muttered through gritted teeth. "I'll take the dog. But the instant I find my brother, she's his responsibility."

Dani clapped her hands together and treated me to the full force of her doe eyes. "Thank you so much, Angel. You won't regret it. Bernice will be on her best behavior."

Having seen Bernice in action, I suspected that what passed for her best behavior wouldn't bring me joy. However, I'd committed to chaperoning the furry beast for the day. Maybe she'd earn her keep by picking up my brother's scent and helping me to find him. But how much mayhem would she cause in the process?

## 13

*A*rmed with poop bags and attitude, I marched out of the villa's gates. Bernice was thrilled to be on the move. It had particularly delighted her when I'd let her crotch-sniff Chief Inspector Colombo. He'd still been loitering in the courtyard when I left Dani's apartment and hadn't been pleased when I untied the dog and let her loose. The memory of his outraged expression brought a smile to my face and a spring to my step.

Across the street from Villa Margherita, an elderly lady made a show of trimming her hedge, keeping a close eye on the Murder House all the while. I summed up the situation with one swift glance. Here was a classic example of a nosy neighbor. The sort of old lady who trained binoculars on her neighbors and kept meticulous mental records of their comings and goings. She was also the type who liked to gossip when given the chance. Although my priority was rescuing my brother, solving the murder would remove me from the police's suspect list. I tugged on Bernice's leash and crossed the road.

"Good morning, *signora,*" I said cheerfully.

"Good morning." The woman eyed me with interest and petted Bernice.

To my relief, the dog didn't jump on her. Clearly, Bernice knew this lady and treated her with respect. I followed Bernice's lead. "I suppose you've heard about the murder."

Her wrinkled face grew animated. "Isn't it awful? I have several of Lucky Lucchese's mysteries on my bookshelves, most of them signed copies. I haven't read all of them, but I have read the series set in Cinque Terre. In Italian translation—my English isn't very good."

My heart rate kicked up a notch. "Lucky set books in Cinque Terre?"

"Oh, yes. He was working on the fifth book—the one set in Monterosso—when he was here this summer. I believe it will be released next year."

"So he wrote one book for each of the five towns?"

"Exactly. They're among his most popular books." She leaned closer, and lowered her voice to a stage whisper. "Is it true that the police have arrested Jocelyn?"

"He's currently 'helping the police with their inquiries.'" I made air quotes to emphasize my point.

The grooves on the old lady's forehead deepened. "I can't see Jocelyn killing anyone. At least, not deliberately. Do you think he surprised Lucky in the apartment and panicked? Lucky's never here in winter. Perhaps he gave Jocelyn a fright."

"And then Jocelyn killed him, thinking he was a dangerous intruder?" I frowned, considering this possibility. "Jocelyn insists he didn't see Lucky yesterday. I'm inclined to believe him."

"Jocelyn's an oddball, but there's no harm in him." The woman's pale eyes seemed to see right through me. "I saw you out with the dog yesterday. Barbie tells you me you're Jimmy's sister."

"That's right." I extended a hand. "I'm Angel Doyle—or Kimmy as some people call me."

"Signora Ricci." Her handshake was surprisingly firm for such a frail-looking old lady.

I regarded her house—a smaller residence than Villa Margherita, but charmingly situated in the middle of a garden filled with lemon trees. "Have you lived here long?"

Pride suffused her face. "Nearly fifty years. I moved here when I got married. I renovated the house after my husband died and turned it into four apartments. It's hard to make a pension stretch in this economy."

"With all the work your garden needs, you must see a lot of comings and goings at Villa Margherita. I don't suppose you saw Lucky arrive yesterday?"

Her gaze was shrewd. "The police already asked me that. No, I haven't seen Lucky since he left for the US at the end of September."

"Did you see anything unusual yesterday? Any strangers arriving at the villa?"

She looked amused. "Apart from you? No. A few of the houses on this street have tourist apartments. We're used to seeing strangers. Less at this time of year than in summer, but Monterosso is a popular tourist destination all year round. Why are you asking these questions?"

"Because after Jocelyn, I'm next on the police's suspect list. And, no," I added, catching the unspoken question, "I didn't murder Lucky."

Her shrewd gaze rested on my face for a long moment, making me squirm under her scrutiny. "Your brother and Dani have lived at the villa for a while. Who do they think did it?"

"My brother's away at the moment. I'll have to ask him when he gets back."

She arched an eyebrow. "Another fishing trip? I hope he's not still working for Paolo Moretti."

"You know Paolo?" I failed to disguise the urgency in my question, prompting a thoughtful look from my listener.

"You've heard of Paolo's reputation." It was a statement, not a question.

"I had the joy of making his acquaintance yesterday," I said dryly. "We didn't hit it off."

"Paolo suffers from big fish, small pond syndrome. It's a shame. He was a lovely little boy. He and his twin brother sang in the church choir. Voices like angels." She paused for dramatic effect. "And then their voices broke."

This I took to be a euphemism for the boys simultaneously hitting adolescence and the skids. "Do I need to watch out for Paolo's twin in a matching gray suit?"

"No. Emilio died many years ago. There's only one Moretti twin left now. Frankly, one's more than enough for this town." Her eyes narrowed. "Your brother should steer clear of Paolo. No good ever came from working for that man."

"I'm not sure where my brother is working at the moment." A glimmer of an idea sparked in my mind. "Signora Ricci, when did you last see Jimmy?"

"Yesterday morning." Her reply came without hesitation.

My heart performed a thump and roll. "You saw him leave the villa? What time was this?"

"I saw Jimmy walking by the beach. I don't know the exact time, but it must have been around seven-fifteen. Rollo, my elderly Pekingese, likes continuity. I always take him for his morning walk before breakfast. Jimmy stopped for a chat and to pet Rollo, just like he always does." She regarded me thoughtfully. "He was carrying a bakery bag and said he and Dani were planning a quiet Sunday at home. He never mentioned your visit."

"You didn't see him when you were on your way back from your walk?"

"No. I met Signor Romano walking down the hill with his Scotch terrier. No one else." She drew her brows together. "No, that's not right. There was someone. A stranger. Some sort of tramp. I didn't pay him close attention because Rollo was getting restive."

A tingle of excitement eased some of the tension in my shoulders. "Some sort of tramp? Can you be more specific?"

Signora Ricci considered my question for a moment before answering. "He had a bushy beard. And hair that didn't match. I can't remember what the hairstyle is called. My grandson says that sort of style is cultural appropriation."

It didn't take a feat of mental gymnastics to work out what she meant. "You saw a white man with dreadlocks?"

"Yes, dreadlocks." She beamed at me. "I'd forgotten the word."

"You said the man's beard and hair didn't match. What did you mean?"

"The beard was black, and the hair was light brown. I don't know why anyone would dye their hair and beard different colors."

Had the tramp been wearing a disguise? Perhaps

purloined from Riccardo's costume box? "It seems an unusual choice. How tall was he?"

"I'm not sure." She cocked her head to the side, considering. "Average, maybe? The only other thing I remember about him is that he wore a baggy coat."

"He didn't happen to be carrying a bakery bag by any chance?"

"I don't recall a bakery bag." Her eyes grew flying-saucer wide. "Why are you so interested in this man? Do you think he could be the murderer?"

"I don't know. I'm interested in anyone who could be the killer who isn't Jocelyn or me." My mental processor whirred. "What time did you see this tramp?"

"Shortly before eight. Rollo and I go out for an hour each morning, and we were almost home when I noticed the tramp." Signora Ricci's gaze returned to Villa Margherita. "I can't see why anyone would want to kill Lucky. He wasn't a nice man, but murdering him seems extreme."

"You didn't like him? Why?"

"He was arrogant. He never wasted an opportunity to tell people how successful he was. Apparently, his great-grandparents came from this area before they emigrated to the United States. Lucky enjoyed lording it over the locals." She pursed her lips in disapproval. "Some people treated him like a celebrity, and he grew to expect that from everyone. It's a shame because his books are wonderful. I've learned to separate the author from the man so that I can continue to enjoy them."

"How does Jocelyn compare to Lucky? Is he disliked in Monterosso?"

"I wouldn't describe him as popular with the locals, but there's no harm in him. He's an odd duck and inclined to be paranoid. At least *he* never struts around the town, waiting to be recognized."

"How do other people in this neighborhood feel about Lucky and Jocelyn? Does anyone have a grudge against either man?"

"As I told you, Lucky was arrogant. That's bound to upset people. And Jocelyn can be difficult. Not mean, but cranky. If he latches on to an idea, he won't give up, especially if concerns his privacy. Recently, he had a run-in with my son about our security cameras. He wanted us to point them so that Villa Margherita wouldn't appear on our surveillance footage."

"I bet the police were interested in that argument." As was I. Jocelyn had persuaded his landlord to switch off the villa's security cameras, and his altercation with Signora Ricci's son had resulted in the Riccis angling their cameras away from the villa. Was this a coincidence? Or had Jocelyn known he'd need to be unobserved on Sunday morning?

"Oh, yes. The police spoke to my son first thing this morning. They were calling door-to-door, looking for any security footage in the neighborhood. But we couldn't help them. After Jocelyn threatened us with legal action, my son moved the camera at the front of our house. Now all it records is my garden." Her lips curved into a bemused smile. "Ironic, isn't it? If Jocelyn hadn't insisted we move our camera, we might have had footage that exonerated him."

"Or footage that ensured his conviction." A loaded silence descended for a moment until I broke it with a fresh question. "What do you think of the other people living at Villa Margherita?"

She screwed up her nose. "I don't think much of Ken. He's too stuck-up for my tastes. His girlfriend is nice, though. She always stops to chat. I like Saul and Riccardo, the gay couple who live upstairs. I occasionally play canasta with Maria Bianchi from apartment four. Your brother's a rogue, but I like him. Out of all the permanent residents at Villa Margherita, I know Dani the least. I believe she's been on bed rest for the last few months. She hardly ever leaves the villa."

"The baby is due in a few days. Hopefully, she'll be able to get around more after the birth." Bernice, who'd been conducting a sniff-check on the pavement, grew bored and tugged on her leash. "I'd better get moving before she makes a bid for freedom."

"It was nice talking to you, dear. I'm sorry this awful murder blighted your visit to Monterosso." She clicked her teeth together. "Such an unpleasant thing to happen."

Unpleasant was an understatement, especially

since the murder investigation was impeding my efforts to find my brother and get to Florida. Preoccupied with digesting my conversation with Signora Ricci, I allowed Bernice to set the pace down the hill. Assuming she hadn't mixed up her days of the week, Signora Ricci had met Del yesterday morning, right about the time it would have taken for him to walk from Marco's apartment to the villa. Yet Dani denied seeing Del yesterday. And if he'd bought baked goods on his way home, surely she'd have mentioned finding them in their apartment?

So what happened to my brother after his chat with Signora Ricci? Had he made it back to the villa? If so, why had Dani not seen him? And was the timing of Del's disappearance connected with the murder? Lucy Carrington had estimated that Lucky died between three and seven on Sunday morning. Had Del discovered his body and then scarpered? Or, worse still, had Del killed Lucky, either by accident or by design?

It wasn't a great leap of the imagination to guess that Del had been the mismatched tramp Signora Ricci had spotted on her way back from her walk. It sounded like the sort of silly costume Del would pick. But if my brother was Signora Ricci's tramp, what had he done with the bakery bag?

The memory of Dani's chocolate croissants loomed large. Could they have been among the baked goods my brother purchased yesterday morning? The croissant I'd tasted had seemed fresh, but I'd soon lost my appetite when my conversation with Dani took a bad turn.

Maybe the croissants were from yesterday, and she'd simply warmed them up in the oven. Dani claimed she had difficulties getting around, so surely she hadn't gone out to a bakery herself? But if Del had purchased the croissants, why hadn't Dani mentioned finding a bakery bag in their apartment yesterday morning?

Assuming Signora Ricci's story was true, there had to be a connection between my brother's kidnapping and Lucky Lucchese's murder. It was time for me to join forces with Sidney and get to the bottom of both mysteries.

## 14

*A*fter a fruitless attempt to track down Del's friends Marco and Alessandro, I texted Sidney and arranged to meet him for a late lunch at one of the few places open at two in the afternoon— Arturo's Gelateria. Arturo and Paolo Moretti sat at the same table they'd occupied yesterday, drinking espressos and playing chess. They ignored me, and I was content to be ignored, choosing a table as far away from theirs as possible.

While I waited for Sidney to arrive, I ordered food and water for Bernice and used my internet research skills to dig for info on Dani, Jocelyn, and Lucky. Dani was easy to find under her married name. Three years ago, a glossy celebrity magazine had featured her wedding to Luigi, complete with a loved-up interview with the happy couple. Dani glowed in her wedding photographs, sleekly confident in a diamond-studded designer dress.

According to the magazine feature, Dani's father was Franco Locatelli, a wealthy industrialist from Milan. I didn't find any connection between Franco and the Mafia, but I placed little reliance on a cursory internet search. Dani and her sister had attended exclusive boarding schools and had jettisoned third-level education to become social media influencers.

Dani had last updated her social media profiles several months before she'd absconded with my brother. Scrolling through her flawlessly filtered photos was like flipping through the pages of a travel brochure. Luigi and Dani—or Anna-Sofia as she'd been known then—had lived the high life in exotic locations around the world. However badly Luigi had treated Dani behind the scenes, I found it hard to imagine that a woman used to such luxury could find long-term happiness with my brother. Even in the unlikely event that Dani persuaded Del to go straight, he'd never bring home the sort of money her father and Luigi had in abundance.

Lucky was equally easy to internet stalk. His author website was a self-congratulatory lovefest featuring photos of Lucky posing outside various government agency buildings, shaking hands with politicians, and breaking bread with known Italian-American mobsters. An internet search brought up pages of links to interviews Lucky had done in print, audio, and for TV. He was famous for writing fast-paced crime novels loosely based on real-life crimes. The twists and turns and colorful characters made them perfect fodder for small- and large-screen adaptations. Despite the plethora of information about Lucky, the writer, details about his private life were surprisingly scant. The internet recorded his age as sixty-two and indicated he had a couple of ex-wives who refused to be interviewed. I found no mention of children.

Of my three research suspects, Jocelyn was the hardest to find. After consulting several forums devoted to conspiracy theories, I found a blog allegedly run by Jocelyn, albeit under a pseudonym. I couldn't find his author website, but then, he probably used a different pseudonym for his books. I'd have to ask Sidney for more details about his cousin.

By the time Sidney walked into the ice cream parlor, Bernice was enjoying an afternoon snooze, and I was on my second double espresso. Instead of his usually perfect posture, his shoulders were hunched, and he looked exhausted.

He slumped into a chair and perused the menu. "They have sandwiches as well as ice cream. I'm going to start with something savory, then move on to sweet."

"I'll do the same. I'm starving. When you arrived, I was on the verge of ordering food."

He glanced up from his menu. "Didn't you eat at Dani's place?"

"Just a couple of bites of a chocolate croissant. The conversation took an uncomfortable turn, and I lost my appetite."

"You need to eat, Angel. You can't run around town looking for your brother on an empty stomach."

"Right back at you. When was the last time you ate?"

He flashed me a rueful smile. "Last night. Jocelyn called right after you left the hotel and I ended up skipping breakfast."

Barbie approached our table, her trademark cheery smile in place. "Hey, there. Are you ready to order?"

Sidney barely registered her sex-shop uniform, but his eyes bugged out when he reached her face. "Trudi Taylor? You *are* Trudi Taylor, aren't you? Who played Bonnie-Rae Gibbons in *Surfer Bay*?"

Barbie's grin was positively radioactive. "That's right. Trudi is my stage name. Fancy you recognizing me. So few people do after my weight loss."

"I'm a huge *Surfer Bay* fan," Sidney gushed, "but the soap hasn't been the same since your character went to live on Planet Zog. I adored Bonnie-Rae's body positivity."

"Surfer Bay? Planet Zog? What the—?" I looked at Sidney for enlightenment.

"It's a long story," Sidney said.

Barbie nodded sagely. "Very convoluted. As you've probably gathered, I was an actor in an Aussie soap for a few years. Until my character eloped with an alien."

I looked from one to the other. "You're not pulling my leg?"

Sidney shook his head. "No, I swear, Angel. Basically, Bonnie-Rae fell in love with her brother-in-law, Lance, played by the incomparable Jake Jones. Only Lance turned out to be the lost prince of Planet Zog. During his time on our planet, he attended Surfer Bay High and married Sookie Phillips."

"And underwent a sex change," Barbie added.

"And then reversed said sex change," Sidney continued. "After all that, Lance's people arrived in their spaceship to rescue him."

"When they finally found him, he was about to elope with my character, Bonnie-Rae. My storyline ended when Lance took Bonnie-Rae captive on his spaceship. They blasted off to Planet Zog and haven't been seen since." Barbie shifted her gum to her other cheek. "Which translates to: the actor who played Lance went to rehab, and I was shipped off to a weight loss facility to help me transition to other roles."

I opened and shut my mouth, carp-like. "There are no words."

"Yes, there are." Sidney turned doe eyes to Barbie. "Will you please pose for a selfie with me? It'd make my year."

Barbie was delighted. "I'd be honored. I rarely meet fans these days."

Several snaps later, we got around to actual introductions.

"This is Sidney," I said. "Jocelyn's cousin."

Barbie batted her caterpillar eyelashes. Sidney had that effect on people. He was charm personified and utterly devoid of the arrogance that so often accompanied it. "When I'm not acting, I'm Barbie, Jocelyn's neighbor. Nice to meet you, Sidney. Is your cousin still at the police station?"

Sidney shook his head. "The police released him an hour ago. They don't have enough evidence to charge him with the murder."

The girl's smile faded. "Does that mean he'll come back to the villa? No offense, but I don't like the idea of living downstairs from a murder suspect."

"His apartment is still a designated crime scene," Sidney reassured her. "He'll stay with me at my hotel until he can get back into his apartment."

Her relief was palpable. "That's probably for the best. No one at the villa wants to see him at the moment."

"So much for 'innocent until proven guilty,'" I said dryly. "The police also brought me in for questioning. Am I equally unwelcome at Villa Margherita?"

Barbie's flush turned her pale skin beetroot. "The villa's a peaceful place. We're not used to violence. I loved living there until yesterday evening."

"I'm sorry this happened in your home," I said, "but it's not my fault."

"And I don't believe it's Jocelyn's fault, either," Sidney added.

"Don't you see that makes it even worse?" Barbie gnawed at her lower lip. "If Jocelyn's innocent, that means the killer is still at large. What if he comes back?"

"The police have a guard on the gate," I pointed out.

"And I overheard at the police station that your landlord has switched back on the security cameras," Sidney said. "The villa is probably the safest place you can be at the moment."

Barbie hugged herself, making me sure the straining bodice of her dress would burst open. "I didn't sleep a wink last night. Ken and I tossed and turned until we gave up, got up, and watched a rom-com."

"What about the night before last?" I asked. "Did you and Ken see or hear anything strange? The police think Lucky was killed between three and seven in the morning."

She shook her head. "No, but then we wouldn't have. Ken was at a conference in Milan on Saturday and crashed at a coworker's place. I took the opportunity of a rare night alone to watch K-dramas and drink too much wine."

Sidney's stomach growled, breaking the tension and making us all laugh. "Are you still serving sandwiches?" he asked.

"Yeah, We have wraps, toasted sandwiches, and bruschetta."

"Do you want to split a bruschetta platter?" Sidney asked me. "And maybe a mixed salad?"

"Sure. That sounds perfect."

Barbie scribbled down our order and retreated to the kitchen. When she was gone, Sidney glanced around the ice cream parlor. Apart from Arturo and Paolo, the place was empty. "Is it safe to talk here?" he whispered.

"Within limits." I inclined my head in the direction of the chess players. "I have a story about one of them, but it'll keep for later."

For the next twenty minutes, we drank coffee and ate the best bruschetta I'd ever tasted. While we ate, I filled Sidney in on my morning's discoveries. I kept my voice low, but neither the old men nor Barbie showed any inclination to eavesdrop on our conversation. "That's why," I said in conclusion, "I think my brother returned to the villa early yesterday morning."

"And left soon after?" Sidney sat back in his chair and pondered what I'd just told him. "What sort of time frame are we talking about?"

"Signora Ricci thinks it was around seven-fifteen when she saw Del down by the beach, and close to eight when she saw the tramp. It takes less than twenty minutes to walk from the beach to the villa. Let's say Del got to the house at seven-thirty-five. Assuming he was the tramp, that means he was at the villa for twenty minutes, max."

Sidney frowned. "Would that give him enough

time to kill Lucky, strip him, and hide the body? And then find a disguise?"

"Maybe? But even if Del killed Lucky, he can't have moved the body into Jocelyn's living room. Jocelyn says he went across the hall to Saul and Riccardo's apartment at six-fifteen. What time was it when you discovered the body?"

"Around six-thirty, or six-thirty-five?" His forehead creased. "I didn't check my watch. You and the dog arrived seconds after I found him."

"That leaves twenty minutes for the killer to smuggle Lucky's body into Jocelyn's apartment." I tapped a finger against the tabletop in a restless rhythm. "Assuming the person who moved the body was the killer."

"And assuming they worked alone," Sidney added. "Jocelyn says the doctor estimated Lucky was killed between three and seven on Sunday morning. That means he'd been dead twelve to sixteen hours when we found him. Wouldn't rigor mortis have set in by then? Could one person have dragged the body to Jocelyn's place without help?"

"I don't know." I heaved a sigh and rubbed my sore temples. "None of this makes sense. Why did the killer plant the body in Jocelyn's apartment? They must have known the lack of blood would make it obvious he hadn't been murdered there."

"Perhaps they didn't care," he suggested. "They needed to move the corpse from wherever they'd hidden it after the murder. Given Jocelyn's apartmentshare-arrangement with the victim, the killer decided he was the perfect person to frame."

I blew out my cheeks and groaned. "This situation is getting more complicated by the second. And that's before we add in our P.I. boot camp mess."

Sidney raised an eyebrow. "No word from your mother?"

"Not a peep."

"On the plus side, at least we know now your brother's kidnapping and the murder must be linked."

"Yeah, but we still don't know why, or who's behind all this." I glanced out the window at the clear blue sky. "We only have a couple more hours of daylight left today. I want to take one of the hiking routes to see if I can spot any likely hiding places for the kidnappers."

"I'll go with you." Sidney drew two brochures out of his jacket pocket. "I stopped by the tourist information office and picked up maps."

"What about Jocelyn? Don't you need to stay in Monterosso to help him?"

"Nah. He's busy with his lawyer. Besides, if the kidnapping and the murder are connected, I'll be helping him by helping you. Speaking of Jocelyn, he and I will be roommates until he can get back into his apartment." Sidney pulled a keycard out of his pocket and handed it to me. "I booked the room next to ours for you."

"Thanks, but I'll need to talk to the hotel manager about Bernice." I glanced down at the snoozing dog. "I let myself be manipulated into looking after her until we find my brother."

"Shouldn't be an issue. I saw a woman check in with a dog when I was leaving this morning."

"That's a relief. I'm not thrilled to have a dog in tow, but at least we'll have a place to sleep tonight."

Sidney leaned down to check out the massive furball at my feet. "That is an enormous dog. Why can't Dani keep her?"

"She's looking after Jocelyn's cats. As we saw yesterday, Bernice loves cats, and they don't reciprocate her enthusiasm."

Sidney slipped his wallet out of his pocket. "We'd better pay and get moving. We should have enough time to hike the trail from Monterosso to Vernazza before it gets dark. The brochure says it takes ninety minutes, and my weather app estimates sunset at five p.m. If we don't find your brother today, we can walk the trail from Vernazza to Corniglia tomorrow."

I motioned for Barbie to bring us the bill. The instant I pushed back my chair and grabbed my jacket, Bernice was wide awake and ready to go. I petted her furry head, and she rewarded me with a generous lick.

"Do you want gelato to go?" Barbie called from behind the counter. "I can add it to your bill before I print it."

The mention of gelato sent Sidney bouncing over

to the gelato display like a jack-in-the-box let loose. Bernice lumbered after him, placing her paws on the display window to check out the selection.

"Do you want some gelato, Angel?" Sidney asked over his shoulder. "They have a white chocolate flavor."

"Sounds delicious, but not right now. Maybe when we get back from Vernazza."

While Sidney debated between a cone and a cup, I dug my notepad and pen out of my backpack. I scribbled my name and phone number and tore the paper free from the pad.

Paolo Moretti didn't look up when I approached his table, but his back stiffened.

Arturo's stern features broke into an unexpectedly cheeky smile. "I hope you and your friend enjoyed your meal."

"We did, thanks." I dropped the slip of paper in front of Paolo. "Yesterday evening, I asked you about my brother. I'm aware of his tendency to get people's backs up, and I have no doubt he was a less than satisfactory employee. Thing is, I believe he's in danger. If you know anything that can help me find him, please contact me."

Paolo's granite gaze raked me from head to toe. "You were at the police station last night."

"Not willingly. You've heard about the murder at Villa Margherita?"

Arturo guffawed with laughter. "Who hasn't? In this town, gossip spreads faster than the clap."

"Did you kill Lucky?" Paolo delivered the question with a sneer. "Or did your brother? The timing of Jimmy's disappearance seems suspicious."

His words rattled me, but I refused to give him the satisfaction of seeing he'd gotten under my skin. Either Marco had spread the word that my brother was missing, or the police had let it slip. "I found Lucky's body, but I didn't know him. Had either of you met him during one of his stays in Monterosso?"

Paolo shook a generous helping of sugar into his espresso cup. "Everyone met Lucky. Lucky made sure of that. The man had a raging ego and was convinced we all worshipped the ground he walked on."

"You didn't like him, then?"

The two men exchanged looks I couldn't read.

"No one liked Lucky," Arturo said. "He pretended to get pally with the locals and then wrote caricatures of them into his books. He had a reputation for mining people for his fiction wherever he went."

"Including people from Monterosso? I understand he'd published books set in the other Cinque Terre towns and was working on the installment set in Monterosso when he died."

Arturo spread his palms wide. "I don't know anything about that. I prefer the classics to crime fiction. All I know is people in the other towns were upset because Lucky had lampooned them in his books."

"Which is a matter of opinion," Paolo added, toying with a rook from the chessboard. "Others loved being included in Lucky's books and considered it a great honor."

I looked from one man to the other, uncertain whether to trust their sudden confidences. "Did anyone sue him for libel?"

"Nah. Nothing like that," Paolo said, deadpan. "Just a few unhappy politicians. The odd disgruntled business owner. And scores of bitter ex-lovers—Lucky got around."

"It sounds like Lucky was a man who liked to make enemies."

Paolo gave a lazy half-shrug. "He got himself murdered. Says it all, doesn't it?"

I tapped a fingertip against the slip of paper I'd dropped in front of him. "If you think of anything that could help me find my brother, please call me. The sooner I find him, the sooner we'll be leaving Monterosso."

Paolo regarded me through hard, expressionless eyes, and a sneer stretched across his craggy face. "I doubt you want to hear from me, little girl. Best you go home and don't interfere in men's business."

White hot anger burned a path from my chest to my throat. Before I had the chance to deliver a blistering retort, Sidney's hand clamped around my arm. "Time to go, Angel."

I itched to wipe the condescending smirk off Paolo Moretti's face, but I had to keep my eyes on the prize. Finally, I had a solid lead on the murder, and, hopefully, on Del's kidnapping. Lucky Lucchese had penned a series of crime novels set in Cinque Terre. Lucky had made himself unpopular with the residents. Had one of them ended his life? If so, I had to find out who. The killer's identity had to hold the key to my brother's kidnapping. I'd come to Monterosso to help Del. If I wound up behind bars for punching Paolo, I'd risk Del's life and my future.

Holding my head up high, I pivoted to leave. Bernice chose that moment to stop in front of Paolo's table, grunt, and release fumes so noxious I thought I'd faint. Leaving Paolo and Arturo literally gagging, the three of us made our exit.

## 15

"I'm starting to like that dog," Sidney said as we hurried down the pavement and away from the scene of the scent. "She chose an excellent moment to let rip."

"Bernice doesn't like Paolo Moretti. I noticed that when we tracked him down yesterday." Once we were a safe distance from the gelateria, I filled Sidney in on my encounter with Moretti at Pepe's bar and my suspicions that he might be involved in Del's kidnapping.

"Have you been able to talk to his nephew yet? The one who's friendly with your brother?"

"Ah, the elusive Alessandro. I've left him several messages, but he hasn't called me back, even though I said my brother was in danger." I wrinkled my nose. "Del never could pick friends. He always finds people who get him into trouble or betray him when he gets himself into trouble."

We crossed the street to the side next to the beach. The warmer weather had attracted a gang of paddling kids, supervised by two bored-looking teenagers. Bernice showed an inclination to join them in the foam, but I held tight to her leash. The last thing I needed was a wet, sandy dog.

Sidney took a spoonful of gelato and moaned in pleasure. "You're missing out. This is the best ice cream I've ever tasted. The cappuccino flavor tastes exactly like a good cappuccino, and the dark chocolate is divine. I regret not getting a third scoop."

I absorbed his ecstatic expression with amusement. "I foresee a daily pilgrimage to Arturo's while we're in the area."

"*Twice* daily. This is a once-in-a-lifetime culinary pleasure. I intend to try as many flavors as I can manage. Meeting *the* Trudi Taylor there is an added bonus."

"I'm still reeling at your description of that *Surfer Bay* plot. However, at least some good has come out of our being in Monterosso. Awesome gelato, your favorite soap star, and blissful views." I tore my attention away from the glimmering blue-green sea and checked my phone. "Still no word from my mother. No doubt she's fuming."

"I can't say I blame her," Sidney said between mouthfuls of gelato. "We'll probably owe her money after this. I doubt she'll get reimbursed for our places in the boot camp."

"I know. I feel awful for skipping out, but what was I to do when Del contacted me in a panic? He's still my brother, even if he's an idiot. I couldn't ignore his plea for help."

Sidney squeezed my shoulder. "I understand. I'd have felt the same way if it were my sister in trouble."

"From what you've told me about your family, your sister isn't likely to get into the sort of pickle that Del regularly finds himself in."

A look of gloom replaced Sidney's sunny smile. "True. She's my parents' golden child, and she's produced three golden grandchildren. Whereas I'm the ne'er-do-well who dropped out of his law course after one miserable semester and switched to drama school. Still," he said, switching back to his cheerful self, "all those acting lessons come in handy during our investigations. It was excellent training for going undercover and persuading people to confide in me."

We neared the outcropping of rock that signaled the end of the sandy beach. A colorful sign proclaimed the start of the famous Cinque Terre Azure Trail, complete with its UNESCO cultural heritage status.

I surveyed the map underneath the sign. "What did the tourist office tell you about the various hiking trails? Are they difficult? I'm confident Bernice can manage anything, but I'm less optimistic about me. My legs are in bits after she walked me yesterday."

"Some trails are more challenging than others, but they're all doable for people with a reasonable fitness level." He produced one of his brochures and spread it open on a nearby bench. "The Azure Trail connects all five towns of Cinque Terre, but only the routes between Monterosso and Vernazza, and Vernazza and Corniglia are open at present. The rest of the trail is closed due to a landslide. We can't rule out that your brother is being held in the closed area, but the lady at the tourist office said it's almost impossible to get down there at the moment, even for locals."

"In that case, we'll focus on the areas that are easily accessible." I traced a finger over the map. "I see train lines here. Are they still running to the towns cut off by the landslide?"

"Yeah. Trains and ferries still stop at Manarola and Riomaggiore. The ferries stop everywhere except Corniglia, which has no harbor. The train covers all five towns."

"We'd get different views from the train, ferry, and walking the trails, even if we're more likely to spot a deserted hut while walking. It's worth trying all three if we don't get lucky on our hikes."

Sidney consulted the brochure. "The trains run regularly, and it's a five to ten-minute run between each town. The ferries don't run as frequently at this time of year. Jocelyn mentioned he keeps a boat in the harbor. We can ask him to take us sailing later today or tomorrow—assuming Chief Inspector Colombo doesn't arrest him in the meantime."

I pointed at the small print on the information poster. "There's a day pass that covers train travel and the hiking trails. Do you think it's worth getting one?"

"It's probably worthwhile getting a two-day pass. We won't cover much ground today before it gets dark."

I conducted a last-minute food and water check before we walked up the stone path to the ticket booth. I wasn't used to having a dog, and I wanted to make sure I had enough supplies to cater to Bernice's prodigious appetite. Apart from her boundless energy and over-enthusiasm for strangers, Bernice was a good dog. She trundled along to the ticket booth, waited patiently for us to buy our two-day passes, and was delighted when we finally got moving on the first section of the hiking trail.

Fifteen minutes into the hike, my thighs were on fire. After a meandering footpath, the trail led to a series of massive stone steps next to lush foliage and rivulets of water. Some steps were so steep that I had to use my hands to drag myself up to the next one. Sidney and Bernice had less trouble with the climb, but the dog gratefully accepted a drink from her water bottle while I got my breath.

"What was it you said about this hiking trail?" I demanded between gasps. "Moderately challenging? Please tell me it gets easier. I don't think I can keep this up for another fifteen minutes, let alone the hour we have left until we reach Vernazza. I'm still bruised and battered after our insane Alpine weekend."

Sidney grinned down at me, looking annoyingly sweat-free. "According to the brochure, the first twenty to thirty minutes of this trail are the hardest. We'll continue to climb for a bit after we reach the top of the steps, but the incline won't be as steep."

I returned the water bottles to my backpack. "Those last few steps were massive. If this continues, you'll have to haul me to the top."

"Consider it good training for the P.I. boot camp," Sidney said cheerfully. "You'll be fine."

"Yeah, right," I snorted. "At the rate our investigation is progressing, we'll never make it to Florida."

"If we don't, we'll find another training course—with or without your mother's financial assistance."

I cocked an eyebrow. "Speak for yourself. My bank account doesn't contain enough to reimburse the Omega Group for the Florida boot camp, never mind fund a second course."

"I'm confident we'll find a way." Sidney reached down to grab my hand. "Let me pull you up the next few steps."

With Sidney's assistance, I scrambled up the next ten steps. After that, the going got considerably easier for a while. The last few steps were rough, but once we crested the top of the stone staircase, the view literally took my breath away. Vines, lemon trees, and olive groves surrounded us. The grapes and lemons had already been harvested, but the olive trees were laden with fruit, and harvesting was in full swing. A local man caught me goggling at their work. He said something in Italian that I didn't catch, cut an olive branch, and tossed it in my direction.

For once, my poor hand-eye coordination didn't let me down, and I caught the branch one-handed. "Grazie," I called. I pulled off an olive and popped it into my mouth. An explosion of taste made me momentarily forget the reason we were on this hike. "Whoa, Sidney. This is pure heaven. Here, try one."

He took an olive and tasted it, nodding in vigorous approval. "Not as fantastically fabulous as my gelato, but still seriously delicious. We need to find your brother and crack the murder case fast. If we stay too long in Cinque Terre, my weight will balloon with all the great food."

Now that we were past the dreaded stone steps, the path curved upward at a more sedate pace. Informational checkpoints provided the history of the Cinque Terre national park and gave details of its flora and fauna. The farther we walked, the more frequent the views of the sea. I knew from my research on the drive to Italy that the hiking trails were the old mule trails used for centuries by the residents.

I kept my eyes peeled for abandoned buildings. All we saw were scattered cottages, obviously occupied, and farm buildings, also in use. We passed several more groups busy with the olive harvest, but we didn't see many fellow hikers until we'd begun the descent into Vernazza.

During our hike, Sidney snapped photos of all the buildings we passed, just in case we missed something important. He paused now at the top of the flight of steps down to Vernazza and happy-sighed. "I know we're on a mission, and this view isn't likely to help us find your brother, but I have to capture this scene."

The view was spectacular.

The town of Vernazza rolled down the slope to a crescent-shaped harbor. Castello Dorio loomed on the far side of the harbor, perched high on the cliff. On the other side, the soft yellow outline of the church of Santa Margherita d'Antiochia drew the eye.

Bernice pulled me down the roped path that led to the harbor square. Tourists gathered on the pier, waiting for the ferry. People spilled out of the church and filed up the slope to the main street. We followed the crowd, passing brightly colored buildings, and pausing in front of tempting shop displays of spices, olives, pesto sauces, and local pottery.

Sidney succumbed to the lures of a spice shop, emerging with a wide grin and a shopping bag. "Spices and information. This is my kind of investigation. I'll hit up that pottery place across the street. It looks like the sort of shop that attracts locals and tourists. Want to set a time to meet? Maybe in forty minutes at the train station?"

"Sure. You concentrate on clothes and pottery. I'll stop by a few restaurants and wineshops."

We parted company, and Bernice and I got busy schmoozing the locals. While schmoozing would never rank high among my talents, I soon discovered that having a shaggy dog as a companion was an excellent icebreaker. At each place we stopped, Bernice played up to our victims, encouraging them to shower her with attention and snacks. I was pretty sure I sucked as a dogsitter for allowing her to graze, but our partnership was a temporary situation.

Lucky's murder was *the* hot topic in Vernazza. Everyone knew who Lucky was, even if they hadn't met him. Several local stores and restaurants stocked his books because he'd featured them in one of his stories, and proudly boasted signs proclaiming their businesses were Lucky Lucchese-approved.

Vernazza was a treasure trove of goodies, even for a jaded tourist like me. I resisted the urge to buy all around me, especially in the bakeries and wineshops. My resolve remained intact until I entered a wineshop, or enoteca, at the end of town, close to the train station. I tied Bernice up outside, not trusting her around the glass bottles.

Enoteca di Lusso was set back from the street, with a grass-covered roof, and an entrance reminiscent of a hobbit hole. When I walked through its round wooden door, I instantly felt out of place, wishing I had Bernice to act as a go-between, yet knowing I'd made the right decision to leave her outside. The shop screamed expensive, with gorgeous carved wine shelves and no discernible price tags. I shuddered to think how much havoc she could cause in here.

Apart from an exquisitely dressed silver-haired woman arranging a wine-tasting display, the shop was empty. She straightened when she saw me and greeted me with unexpected warmth. She gestured to the display. "Would you like to sample some of our local wines?"

I pushed past the fish-out-of-water sensation. "Yes, please. I'd love to."

My host guided me through six separate wine samples—four white and two red—and all served in exquisite wine glasses. All my previous experiences of wine-tastings involved thimble-sized plastic cups. By the fifth wine sample, we were on first-name terms, and I'd nudged the conversation toward the murder.

"Yes, I knew Lucky, but we weren't friends." Vanessa pursed her scarlet-painted lips. "To tell the truth, we had a disagreement a couple of years ago. He promised to feature my enoteca in his Vernazza mystery. We even got as far as negotiating the fee—"

"A fee?" I burst out. "He wanted to charge you for the privilege of appearing in his book?"

"Oh, yes." Vanessa's mouth twisted into a smile. "With Lucky, it was a pay-to-play arrangement. And to be fair, the businesses he put in his books became tourist attractions. Have you seen all the displays of his work in shops that don't otherwise sell books? Including both the English originals and the Italian translations? Every one of those businesses paid for a mention in a Lucky Lucchese mystery."

"You said you got as far as negotiating a fee with Lucky. What went wrong?"

"It was more a case of *who* went wrong." Vanessa waved her scarlet-tipped fingers. "Matteo Parodi owns Enoteca Parodi down by the harbor, and he has a seat on the local council. He approached Lucky with an offer to double the fee I'd offered. The deal was contingent on Lucky agreeing not only to feature Enoteca Parodi in his book *Vanished in Vernazza* but also to write Matteo into the story."

I took another sip of wine number five, a Vernaccia made from grapes grown in the hills above Vernazza, and my favorite so far. "Did the deal work out for Matteo?"

Vanessa burst out laughing. "If you mean, did he make money, then yes. In abundance. His enoteca is strategically placed to be seen by everyone getting off the ferry, and there's a vast display of *Vanished in Vernazza* in the shop window under a 'Lucky Lucchese-approved' plaque. All signed, of course—by Lucky's Italian assistant."

"From your laughter, I take it there was a flip side

for Matteo. What happened? Did Lucky parody him in the book?"

"So you've heard about Lucky's tendency to poke fun at the locals he used as inspiration for the characters in his series?" Vanessa's grin widened, exposing her slight overbite. "In Matteo's case, it went further than poking fun. Lucky exposed his affair with his sister-in-law, ending two marriages and causing a political scandal Matteo barely slithered free from. Matteo couldn't sue for libel because Lucky had written nothing but the truth."

"Ouch. Are there similar stories from the other towns Lucky used in his mysteries?"

"I believe so, but none is as publicly known as Matteo's experience with Lucky." Vanessa poured the sixth wine into a fresh wineglass and handed it to me. "This is Sciacchetrà, a very special wine, the pride of the Cinque Terre. It was known as the gold of the Cinque Terre in the Middle Ages because it was a valuable trade asset. It takes a very long time to make and then it stays good for over twenty years. We have a tradition whereby we gift a bottle to a newborn baby, and then they open the bottle when they're an adult."

I sniffed the rich honey-hued liquid as though I had a clue and then took a sip. It tasted even better than it smelled. I wasn't usually a fan of sweet wines, but this was delicious. Maybe I'd buy a bottle for my soon-to-be niece or nephew. Or for mother as a peace offering.

Inside my jacket pocket, my phone vibrated with an incoming message. A creepy crawly feeling slithered through my insides, making me regret my decision to succumb to a wine-tasting. "I'm sorry, Vanessa, but I have to check my phone."

"No problem. Would you like me to arrange a few bottles for you to choose from?"

"Yes, please. I won't be a sec." Had my mother finally responded with a well-deserved upbraiding? Or had Dani received a third demand from Del's kidnappers?

I slid my phone out of my pocket and swiped the screen. Two missed calls and a text message, all from the same unknown number. I opened the message.

*Call me. Urgent. Love, Dad.*

I choked down a wave of nausea. After the latest ransom demand, I figured I'd have to contact him, but I hadn't expected him to beat me to the punch. After two long years of radio silence, what warranted Dad's sudden urge to speak to me? Did he know about Del's latest hot mess? And was he aware of who was behind the kidnapping?

*S*till reeling from my father's text message, I clinked out of Enoteca di Lusso, carrying one sinfully expensive bottle of Sciacchetrà and three more affordable alternatives. During my time in the shop, the last vestiges of daylight had given way to darkness, and the first restaurants were opening for the evening trade. The glowing lights along Vernazza's main street cast an orange tint over the brightly colored buildings.

Outside the wineshop, Sidney lounged on a bench, giving Bernice a drink of water. I'd seen him look after Mélisandre, our housemate Luc's prissy Persian, but he was adorable with the dog. He'd always claimed to be a dog person, and Bernice was digging the attention.

After the shock of Dad's message, I had to curb the urge to throw myself into Sidney's arms. Where had this newfound need for PDAs sprung from? In public and private, I wasn't a hugger. The events of the last few days had put my equilibrium on a nonstop roller-coaster.

The clink of my newly bought loot drew his attention away from the dog. "I see you've been busy. When I spotted Bernice outside this enoteca, I guessed you were inside, buying the place out. I figured I'd wait for you, and we'd walk to the train station together."

"Excellent deduction, Sherlock." I displayed my purchases. "The expensive wine will be a present. The other three bottles are fair game. And seeing as we're unarmed, at least we can chuck bottles at any would-be attackers."

"I prefer the version where I help you drink the wine, not throw it at villains. After our Swiss weekend, I'm over violence." Sidney returned the dog's water bottle to his backpack and showed me his two carrier bags. "We rock at this investigating business. We combine asking questions with my favorite pursuit —shopping."

"I thought your current favorite pursuit was eating gelato," I teased, untying Bernice's leash.

"Can't a man enjoy both?" Sidney steered us past a sign pointing to the train station. "Slight change of plan, by the way. Jocelyn called while you were knocking back the wineshop's stock. He invited us to meet him for dinner at his favorite seafood restaurant in Corniglia, one town over. He's agreed to clue us in about his mysterious book research."

"A seafood restaurant? Isn't Jocelyn vegan?" That panicky feeling I'd experienced yesterday was back in full force, lending my fingers a prickly numbness that forced me to squeeze the leash tight lest I let it drop. I had an uneasy feeling I was being watched. But hadn't the person tailing me yesterday been Sidney? Who could be following me today?

"Jocelyn's vegan, but he says this place has a decent selection of vegan and non-vegan options. He thought we'd want to try seafood while we're in Cinque Terre. My cousin is a pain, but he's a foodie. If he considers the restaurant good, we can look forward to a slap-up meal." Sidney slid me an appraising look. "You ooze tension. What happened? Did you discover something important?"

I pulled my jacket tight against a cool evening breeze. "Maybe? It concerns a potential motive for Lucky's murder, but I can't see how it can have anything to do with my brother's kidnapping."

By the time we boarded the train to Corniglia and found a carriage with an empty four-seater, I'd supplied Sidney with a comprehensive run-down of my conversation with Vanessa in Enoteca di Lusso, ending my recital with the news of my father's unexpected message.

"That's a lot to unpack," he said when I'd finished. "When we get to Corniglia, do you want to find somewhere quiet to call your father before we meet Jocelyn at the restaurant?"

The tingling, panicky sensation crept over my chest again. I whipped around and scanned the train carriage. No familiar faces. "Ah, no," I said when I slid back into my seat and met Sidney's questioning gaze. "I'll deal with Dad later. I need a good meal first. What did you find out in Vernazza?"

"Not much, although I met Nico, Lucky's part-time assistant."

I perked up at this new info. "Seriously? That was a stroke of luck."

"Nico works at a bookshop on Piazza Marconi, the bookshop featured in Lucky's *Vanished in Vernazza*. I called in to get the low-down on Lucky, and Nico revealed he worked for him part-time as his virtual assistant. He didn't mention Lucky letting him sign books on his behalf, though. However, he confirmed what Vanessa told you about the pay-to-play arrangement with local businesses. That practice caused a few fallings-out among rival business owners."

"I bet it did. I wonder if Nico knows the plot premise of the book Lucky was working on before he died."

"I asked him that question, and he said Lucky was cagey on plot details. All he knows is that the book was called *Murdered in Monterosso*. The research Nico undertook on Lucky's behalf was basic stuff. Checking tides, distances from place to place, and other minor fact-checking. He also arranged meetings between Lucky and business owners in Cinque Terre. However, the bulk of Nico's responsibilities revolved around monitoring Lucky's Italian fan mail, and moderating his Italian fan club."

"Would Nico be willing to talk to us again if we have more questions? If he worked for Lucky, he must have a lot of insider info."

"I took his number, but Nico rarely spoke to Lucky directly. Most of their communication was via email." A triumphant smile stretched across his face. "This brings me to the one interesting nugget I gleaned from our conversation—Lucky's mastery of Italian. Apparently, Lucky insisted on speaking English to everyone, peppering his speech with a smattering of Italian phrases. Everyone assumed he was monolingual. Yet Nico insists Lucky spoke excellent Italian when they discussed his research goals, and his emails in Italian were error free."

I considered this new information. "Why did Lucky refuse to speak Italian with the locals?"

"I don't know. Maybe his insistence on speaking English was part of his public persona. He clearly enjoyed getting people's backs up. Perhaps forcing them to speak English to him was his idea of fun."

The journey from Vernazza to Corniglia took just a few minutes. After we got off the train, a set of steep steps leading from the platform up to the town obliged us to hit the pause button on our conversation. I lost count after I got to three hundred. Let's just say there were a lot of steps. When we reached the top, even Bernice was panting.

I got my bearings and surveyed my surroundings. Corniglia was built on a smaller scale than Vernazza, nestling high on a cliff, overlooking the sea. Like the other Cinque Terre towns, it boasted rows of colorful buildings. It was beautiful at night, but I longed to see the dramatic sea views in daylight. If we stuck to our plan of taking the Vernazza-Corniglia hiking trail tomorrow, I'd get my wish.

The narrow side street Sidney's maps app led us down featured art galleries and shops selling luxury fabrics. "We're early," he said over his shoulder. "The restaurant doesn't open until seven."

I opened my mouth to suggest we use the opportunity to stop and ask questions, but then I saw two familiar figures bumping their way over the cobblestones.

Lucy Carrington's round face was red from the effort of pushing her sister's wheelchair up the incline. She blinked when she recognized me. "Hello, there. Angel, isn't it? Dani said the police had let you go."

"After many painful hours in their company." I gestured to Sidney. "This is Sidney. He's Jocelyn's cousin."

"And this is my sister, Heather." Lucy parked the wheelchair in front of a window resplendent with watercolors of Cinque Terre.

Once the introductions were out of the way,

Sidney exerted himself to make the women feel comfortable and slowly coaxed them out of their shells. "Have you seen much of Cinque Terre so far?"

"We spent the day sightseeing." Heather's tone was soft and tentative, as though she rarely spoke to strangers. "We took the van to Vernazza and Corniglia, and tomorrow we'll take the ferry to the other towns."

"Not all the train stations are wheelchair accessible," Lucy elaborated. "We have a permit to drive our rental van into the towns, but taking the ferry will allow us to see more. Unfortunately, Corniglia has no harbor, so we had to take the van and park on the outskirts of town."

Heather smiled up at her sister. "Poor Lucy. We underestimated just how steep these towns are." Bernice approached Heather's wheelchair, subjecting its wheels to a thorough inspection. The woman stroked the dog's back. "You have a beautiful dog. We met her yesterday evening at the dinner party—before all the unpleasantness."

"She's not our dog," Sidney clarified. "Angel is looking after her for Dani."

"Yes, she mentioned her baby is due soon," Lucy said. "How awful for her to have the stress of a murder in the villa on top of waiting to give birth."

"Dani says she barely knew Lucky," I said. "Still, I agree—it's rotten to have a murderer at large in your building."

Heather's eyes widened in fear. "Surely whoever killed that man is long gone."

"Unless the murderer is one of the other residents," Sidney suggested. "It's odd that Lucky was in Monterosso. He and my cousin share their apartment on a six-month on, six-month off basis. Lucky wasn't due back until April."

"Were you at the villa when the police searched it this morning?" I asked, observing their reactions.

The sisters exchanged glances, but all I could read was discomfort at my probing questions.

"Yes," Lucy replied, "although they didn't need to search the entire villa. They found bloodstains in the basement when they checked last night, and they concentrated on that and the apartment where the body was found."

"Did they question you about your movements yesterday?" I pulled a silly face. "Chief Inspector Colombo knows how to make a person feel special."

This elicited a tight smile from Lucy. "He's not a pleasant person. Yes, he wanted to know what time we moved into our apartment on Sunday, and when we arrived at the potluck."

"We came under particular scrutiny because we're the only people who used the lift," Heather said, pressing her lips into a moue of distaste.

"We're the only people who *admit* to using it," Lucy said pointedly. "As we told the inspector, we didn't use the lift during the time that the body must have been moved from the basement to the apartment.

"That would have been, what?" I pretended to rack my brains for the time. "Between six-fifteen and six-thirty yesterday evening?"

Heather nodded. "That's right. Colombo seemed disappointed to cross us off his suspect list, but we weren't even in Monterosso when the man died."

"When did you arrive at the villa yesterday?" Sidney asked.

"Not until the afternoon. Around three-thirty. Our flight from London didn't arrive in Milan until noon, and then we had to drive to Monterosso."

"When we arrived at the villa, Saul and Riccardo had left an invitation for us to join their dinner party," Heather said with a small smile. "We were tired after the journey, so not having to go out again for dinner was a lovely surprise."

"What time did you get to the party?" Sidney leaned down to pet Bernice, adding a casualness to his question that I knew to be a lie.

"We were just getting into the lift to go up to Saul and Riccardo's flat when Barbie ran down to tell me you were looking for a doctor. I'm afraid I didn't check the time." Lucy squirmed, uncomfortable with the turn our conversation had taken.

"Have you been to this area of Italy before?" I kept the question light, hoping to dispel some of the wariness I sensed from the sisters. "It's my first time in Cinque Terre."

"Ours, too." Lucy laid a hand on her sister's shoulder. "We usually stick to places that are known for being wheelchair friendly, but we've always longed to see the five towns."

"It's gorgeous here," Sidney said. "I only wish I'd come in summer. November's not the month to see Cinque Terre at its finest."

A tremor passed over Heather's face, gone so fast I had to blink to believe it. Why had Sidney's mention of the season alarmed her? In that brief unguarded moment, she'd shown true terror.

"Well," Lucy released the brake on Heather's wheelchair. "We should get moving. We've booked a table at a restaurant in Monterosso."

"I'm glad you enjoyed your first day in Cinque Terre." I raised my hand to wave goodbye, but a display of Lucky Lucchese mysteries in the window of an art gallery snagged my attention. "Hey, I don't suppose either of you has read any of Lucky's mysteries?"

Heather's mouth formed a frightened 'O.' Lucy's knuckles turned white from gripping the handles of the wheelchair.

"No." Lucy's tone was curt. "We hadn't even heard of the man until he was discovered dead. Now, I'm afraid we have to get going. We don't want to miss our dinner sitting."

When they were out of hearing distance, Sidney looked down at me. "What did you make of that?"

"I'm positive those two are hiding something. However, I don't know if their secret has any relevance to Lucky's murder."

Sidney stared after the sisters, now mere dots in the distance. "Isn't it weird that they'd never heard of Lucky Lucchese before yesterday? He's one of those rare authors who's reached household-name status, even among non-readers."

"Weird, but not impossible." I faux-punched him on the arm. "Remember my blissful ignorance about *Surfer Bay* and its wacky alien plots. You couldn't believe I'd never heard of it."

"You have a point." He checked his phone. "It's almost seven. We can head to the restaurant."

"What's the restaurant called?"

Sidney shrugged. "Jocelyn didn't give a name, just an address. My cousin can be tiresome."

We retraced our steps through the narrow alleyways of Corniglia, following the directions on Sidney's phone. In the alleyways populated with eateries, light spilled onto the cobblestones. Elsewhere, many shops were closing for the day, their shopfronts dark.

When we reached a deserted side lane, the app guided us up a flight of steps to what looked like a church door.

I regarded the heavy iron knocker, my pulse

throbbing in my neck. "Are you sure this is the right place, Sidney?"

A shadow detached from the side of the church, revealing itself to be a man dressed in a hooded cloak reminiscent of a monk's habit.

My heart thumped and rolled, and the panicky prickly sensation I'd had on and off since for days morphed into pure adrenaline. After a weekend of being shot at, chased after, and almost blown up, my fight-or-flight instinct was hovering near the surface.

The monk took a step toward me, and I pounced. Using all my strength, I swung my wine bag at his lower body, hitting him neatly between the legs.

## 17

*T*he monk crumpled, clutched his crotch, and collapsed with an agonized roar. This dramatic turn of events excited Bernice. With a loud bark, she leaped on our would-be attacker and pinned him in place with her paws. Any budding hope I'd had of training her to take down our enemies faded when she treated the man to a thorough licking.

Sidney and I approached the fallen monk. I switched on my phone's flashlight while Sidney stretched down and yanked back the monk's hood.

A scrawny individual with a scraggly beard and a greasy comb-over stared back at us through a pair of orange-tinted spectacles, now missing one lens.

"Jocelyn?" Sidney and I cried in unison. "What are you doing here?"

"Meeting you two, as arranged." He dislodged

Bernice and tried to sit. "Are you insane? Why did you attack me?"

Sidney hauled Jocelyn to his feet and brushed down his ridiculous robes. "*I* didn't attack you. You alarmed Angel."

Heat crept up my cheeks, making me glad it was dark. I had kinda jumped the gun. "In my defense, you lured us to a deserted church, then creeped up on us in the dark. I panicked."

"Did you have to panic so hard?" Jocelyn gestured to his crotch. "What did you hit me with? A lead pipe?"

"Wine bottles." I held up the bag for their inspection.

"Did you break any?" Sidney took the bag from me and reached a cautious hand inside. "Whew. All four bottles are still intact."

"Well, isn't that delightful?" Jocelyn's voice dripped sarcasm. "You're worried about wine? I'm worried I'll never be able to pee again. Is this the thanks I get for inviting you out for a nice meal?"

Sidney cocked an eyebrow and pointed at the church door. "Were you planning on feeding us here? Why didn't you just give us the name of the restaurant?"

"And why are you dressed like a medieval monk?" I asked, checking out the outfit. "Did you raid Riccardo's costume box?"

"I might have." Jocelyn rearranged his robes with

dignity. "I'm in disguise because there are spies *everywhere*. Don't you get it? I'm under constant surveillance. And now that I'm a murder suspect, I have to contend with lumbering police officers following me around. All I wanted was to lose whoever's tailing me and speak to you two privately, away from prying eyes and eager ears."

I slow-clapped. "Very poetic. Speaking of tailing people, have you been following us since we got to Corniglia? I had a feeling I was being watched."

Jocelyn's paranoid gaze slid from side to side, seeming to relax when he'd ascertained we were alone. "I tried to get your attention, but you were too busy gossiping with those tourists from the villa."

"We weren't gossiping," Sidney protested. "We were asking the Carrington sisters about the murder. If you want our help to clear your name, Angel and I have to know who came and went from Villa Margherita on the day Lucky died."

"What can those women possibly know about the murder?" Jocelyn scoffed. "They're first-time visitors to Monterosso, and didn't arrive at the villa until after Lucky was killed."

"For a dude who earns his living expounding upon conspiracy theories, you're awfully trusting of strangers," I said. "How do you know it's their first time in Monterosso? And did you actually see them enter the villa at the time they claim they arrived?"

Jocelyn's steel wool eyebrows formed a wiry V. "You think they're lying?"

"Not necessarily. It's my job not to believe everything people tell me. I always seek corroboration."

Bernice, tired of playing with Jocelyn's robe, whined.

Sidney picked up the end of her leash. "I agree with the dog. Can you please take us to the restaurant? I'm starving."

Grumbling about spies, police persecution, and insane women who attacked his man parts, Jocelyn stagger-led us through a maze of dark alleys, eventually stopping at a restaurant on the edge of town. When we walked in, the tantalizing aroma of freshly cooked garlic, herbs, and seafood reminded me of how long ago Sidney and I had shared our bruschetta platter.

The restaurant was in one of those buildings that appear deceptively tiny on the outside but prove larger once you go inside. Old-fashioned red-and-white checked tablecloths draped over wine casks formed tables, and carved wooden stools served as seats. The place brimmed with a clientele that combined locals and tourists—a good sign in my experience.

A waiter with a swarthy complexion and a thick gold chain around his neck greeted Jocelyn by name and led us up two flights of stairs to a private dining room. The walls were adorned with watercolor paintings of Corniglia, similar to those that I'd seen on our tour of the town.

When we were seated and supplied with menus, Jocelyn and Gianni, our waiter and the proprietor of the establishment, made recommendations. As long as I got my fix of seafood linguine, I was happy to be guided by them. Once he'd supplied us with water, wine, and dog bowls for Bernice, Gianni retreated.

Jocelyn raised his wineglass and sniffed the contents approvingly. "This is my favorite rosé from the region. It's made by a winery in Riomaggiore."

I took a sip and moaned in appreciation. "Delicious. Dry yet fruity. How did you find this restaurant? It's my first time having dinner in a private dining room."

"Gianni's son, Junior, helps me with my research. I trust Gianni and his family implicitly. And they just so happen to run the best restaurant in the area." Jocelyn put down his glass and removed his broken glasses.

I felt a stab of guilt. "I'll replace them."

"Don't worry about the glasses. My vision is perfect. I wear them for privacy purposes only." He regarded me shrewdly. "We didn't meet to discuss my choice in eyewear. Sidney filled me in on the basics, but he was hazy on some details. I gather your brother is in some sort of trouble?"

"That's an understatement." I gave Jocelyn a brief run-down of the situation but refrained from any mention of Del's legal name and Dani's mobster ex-husband.

When I was done, Jocelyn reached into the deep

folds of his robes and withdrew a plastic folder containing a sheaf of papers. "Sidney says you two are private investigators."

"We've solved a few cases, but we're not yet licensed." I cast Sidney a rueful smile. "Actually, we're supposed to be attending a training camp in Florida right now. We were on our way to the airport when I got my brother's text message."

"And now you find yourselves mixed up in a kidnapping and a murder, which may or may not be linked. Does that sum up the situation?"

"Comprehensively."

Conversation ceased when Gianni arrived with our starters—*trofie al pesto* for Sidney, minestrone soup for Jocelyn, and crabmeat ravioli for me. He even brought a juicy steak for Bernice. One bite of ravioli, and I was in culinary heaven.

When Bernice finished wolfing down her meal, I added more water to her bowl and supplied her with a blanket to lie on and a chew toy. "That will keep her occupied while we talk. Sidney tells me you want to trade information. What do you want to know? And how can you help us?"

"I need you to help me prove my innocence. I don't trust the police to conduct a thorough investigation. They've decided I'm guilty, and I doubt they'll bother to seriously consider anyone else."

"To be fair, that's not the impression I got from talking to other residents of Villa Margherita," I said between forkfuls of the divine ravioli. "I don't like Colombo, especially not after he made me spend the night at the police station. Yet I don't think he's a slacker."

"I don't know Chief Inspector Colombo well. However, I have the misfortune of knowing his commanding officer." Jocelyn's nostrils flared with ill-concealed anger. "He's the sort of man who's more concerned with currying favor with politicians and celebrities than in doing his job."

"Okay, so you don't trust the cops," I said, washing my ravioli down with a mouthful of wine. "I get it. I'm not a huge fan of the police, either. So what do you believe we can do for you?"

He leaned forward, oblivious to a dollop of minestrone soup clinging to his beard. "I want you to find out who killed Lucky Lucchese."

Sidney, who'd been devoting himself to his food during this exchange, switched his attention from his plate to his cousin. "What do we get in return? Can you help us figure out who kidnapped Angel's brother and where the kidnappers are holding him?"

"I can try." Jocelyn's gaze swiveled toward me. "For what it's worth, I don't think Lucky's death had anything to do with Jimmy's kidnapping."

I slow-blinked. "Why? Who do you think is responsible?"

The corners of his eyes creased in amusement. "I'm sure we could compile a list of all the people your brother has upset since he moved to Monterosso. He's not a bad bloke, but he drinks too much, takes too many drugs, and has terrible taste in friends."

"All true," I said breezily. "I'll add that he's never held down a legit job for more than a few weeks at a time. And he doesn't fare much better with illicit assignments. Now, how do these scathing but accurate assessments of my brother's character help me find him?"

"Are you aware that Jimmy works for a man named Paolo Moretti?"

"I'm aware that he *used* to work for Paolo." I frowned, recalling my two conversations with the odious Paolo. "Have you heard different?"

"The word on the street is that when your brother first moved to Monterosso, he 'helped' Paolo's nephew on fishing trips."

Sidney caught my eye. "Fishing trips where fish aren't the only catch?"

"Exactly. Apparently, Angel's brother accidentally dropped cargo overboard on a recent outing. Paolo Moretti was spitting mad. Jimmy only avoided permanent injury—or worse—by agreeing to work for Paolo for free until he paid off his debt. Given Jimmy's track record of ineptitude, it's not an enormous leap to suppose he screwed up again, and Paolo decided that the only way he'd see that money was by holding Jimmy for ransom."

My starter sat uncomfortably in my stomach.

"That all makes perfect sense. Yet, if that's what happened, why didn't Dani mention Moretti to me? I heard about him through my brother's friend, Marco. "

"Perhaps Dani doesn't know about Jimmy's debt to Moretti," Jocelyn suggested. "Since they moved into the villa, she's barely left the apartment."

"She's had pregnancy complications," I said. "That's probably why."

"I know she's had a difficult pregnancy, but that doesn't explain how nervy she gets. She won't even answer her door unless Jimmy's home. He tells people he got the dog to keep Dani company when he's away. However, I get the impression he hoped Bernice would act like a guard dog."

Sidney and I burst out laughing. "He must have been disappointed," Sidney said. "Bernice loves everybody."

"To come back to Paolo Moretti, you believe Moretti is behind my brother's kidnapping. You could be right. Can you think of any reason Moretti would suddenly double the ransom demand?"

Jocelyn seemed taken aback by this information. "When did he double the ransom?"

I gave him a brief lowdown of Dani's messages from the kidnappers, ending with the most recent demand for fifty thousand euros.

"Paolo Moretti is extremely careful. Everyone in Cinque Terre knows he imports cannabis and cocaine from France, including the police. Yet he's never been caught. Questioned? Yes. Charged? No. I've researched the drug trade for years. Paolo runs a small but lucrative business, importing drugs and distributing them in this region. My best guess is that he moves small amounts, regularly. I doubt whatever cargo your brother accidentally dropped off the fishing boat was worth twenty-five thousand euros, never mind fifty thousand. And if Jimmy had destroyed twenty-five grand worth of product, Moretti would do far worse to him than force him to work for free."

"Why, then, do you think Moretti is demanding a ransom for Angel's brother's safe return?"

Jocelyn didn't answer Sidney's question immediately because Gianni returned with more food. I was temporarily distracted from worrying about my brother by the heavenly aromas. Jocelyn had ordered a vegan lasagne. Sidney received a clay pot filled with swordfish stew. And I got my much-anticipated seafood linguine, served in a wine sauce with swordfish, calamari, mussels, and prawns.

After we'd made suitable noises of appreciation for his culinary genius, Gianni withdrew, and Jocelyn resumed his tale. "The only reason I can see for Paolo Moretti holding your brother for such a ransom is if Moretti knows Jimmy or Dani has the connections to raise that kind of cash fast." Jocelyn lowered his voice. "Did you look through my research material?"

I shook my head. "But I saw your whiteboard before you took all the material down."

"I was tempted to have a rummage," Sidney admitted, "but I left it alone, as promised."

"My next book is an exposé of the British establishment's historical ties to the Mafia," Jocelyn announced, sounding like a mad professor on amphetamines. "Not Mafia alien conspiracies—I only say that to put people off the scent."

I could see a link between highly placed individuals in the UK and the Generos, but I wasn't clear on how Paolo Moretti could be connected. "What does Paolo Moretti have to do with the UK? From your description of his operation, he concentrates on this area."

"Correct. But Paolo's only been in operation for the last twenty years. He moved back to Monterosso after serving a fifteen-year prison sentence..." Jocelyn paused for dramatic effect, "...in the UK."

## 18

*I* sucked air through my teeth, a coil of anger swirling through my veins. "That low-down snake. Paolo told me he didn't speak English."

Jocelyn roared with laughter. "Seriously? Naughty Paolo. His English is excellent."

"What is this trend with people pretending they don't speak languages?" Sidney asked. "First, Lucky, and now, Paolo."

Jocelyn looked surprised. "What language did Lucky pretend not to speak?"

"Italian, apparently. I spoke to his assistant earlier today. He claimed Lucky had excellent Italian."

"I didn't know that. But then, beyond subletting his apartment, I barely knew the man. Villa Margherita's permanent residents knew Lucky a lot better than I did."

"Given how successful Lucky's author career was,

I'm surprised he didn't buy a house in Cinque Terre," I mused. "Villa Margherita is lovely, but surely he could have afforded a villa of his own?"

Jocelyn nodded slowly. "Yeah, I asked him that question when we first discussed me subletting the apartment. He said he preferred to live among people. He hated being alone. Besides, you overestimate his wealth. People always think authors make more than they do. Even a household name like Lucky doesn't have limitless funds. I bet his payday from his Crimeflix deal was more than he earned on all his books put together."

I longed to ask more about how this all worked, but it was getting late and the clock was ticking on finding my brother. "To return to your book research, how is Paolo Moretti connected to the British establishment?"

Jocelyn refilled my wineglass with the excellent white he'd ordered to accompany our main course. "To tell that story, we need to go back thirty-five years. In those days, Paolo and his twin brother, Emilio, worked in London for an Italian gang with ties to the Mafia."

I felt a tingle of excitement. "The Generos? Is that why you had a photograph of Luigi Genero on your whiteboard?"

"Yes, and no. The Moretti twins worked for the now-defunct Amassi gang. The Generos most assuredly have contacts in the upper echelons of the British government and police, but in those days, Gio Genero and his family were merely bit players on the

London scene." Jocelyn traced a fingertip around the edge of his wineglass and laughed. "What you really want to know, Ms. Angel-Kimmy Doyle, is if I figured out your brother's connection to the Generos."

My spine stiffened, steel rod-style. "You know?"

Jocelyn's grin was of the Cheshire Cat variety. "Of course I know. I've been researching Italian gangs in London for the last year. The Generos are currently the top dogs. I've seen photos of Luigi's bride, the beautiful Anna-Sofia. When she suddenly disappeared, rumors abounded, the most popular being that Luigi had murdered her. Imagine my amazement when I came across her at Villa Margherita. And when I met her boyfriend? No words. Your brother and Luigi Genero have little in common beyond a penchant for crime. How did he wind up running away with Anna-Sofia?"

"I'm hazy about the details," I said. "I only learned of their relationship yesterday. My brother—Del is his real name, short for Derek—worked as Luigi's chauffeur. He and Dani—or Anna-Sofia—started an affair. When she discovered she was pregnant with my brother's child, they ran away to Italy to start a new life. Dani's uncle owns the villa and is allowing them to stay there until the baby's born. Now you know as much as I do."

"Tell us more about the Moretti twins," Sidney urged, "and how they relate to your research."

Jocelyn took a drink from his water glass before

continuing his story. "Emilio and Paolo Moretti moved to London in their late teens, fell in with the Amassi gang, and rose in the ranks. Thirty-five years ago, they were involved in a massive bank robbery in central London, complete with hostages. It ended in a shootout with the police, leaving three hostages, two bank robbers, and one passerby dead. That passerby was my father."

My gaze clashed with Sidney's. "Wasn't your father's death a tragic accident?" I asked gently. "Do you have reason to believe that the Moretti twins killed him?"

Jocelyn's headshake was vehement. "Nothing of the sort. A police bullet killed my father. But that policeman wouldn't have fired his weapon had that bank robbery not taken place. Now, can you see why I need to tell this story? To Paolo Moretti and his ilk, collateral damage is irrelevant. Why should he be allowed to live a cushy life on the proceeds of my father's death?"

Sidney placed a hand on his cousin's shaking shoulders. "I understand your anger, Jocelyn, but please tell us more. Angel and I need to understand what we're dealing with if we're to help you."

"Prior to the shootout, the gang smuggled most of the money out of the bank, absconding with a rumored fifteen million pounds. Most of that money has never been recovered."

I let out a low whistle. "That's a lot of dough. I'm

197

sensing that the bank robbery had consequences for the Moretti twins. Is that why Paolo went to prison?"

"Yes. Paolo's brother, Emilio, suffered fatal injuries in the shootout and later died in the hospital. Paolo was also injured, but less severely, and ended up serving a fifteen-year prison sentence for his role in the robbery." Jocelyn's lips twisted into a bitter smile. "The best part: none of the three men convicted spoke a word at their trial. No information on who planned the robbery. Zero clues as to the location of the stolen money."

"I assume Paolo returned to Italy as soon as he was released," I remarked, processing this new information. "Do you think he used some of the stolen money to set up business in Monterosso?"

"One hundred percent. Everyone knew that Paolo and the two other men who were convicted of the bank robbery weren't the masterminds. I believe they received substantial financial compensation after they got out of prison in return for keeping their mouths shut. One man died shortly before his release, and the other has been in and out of prison over the years. Only Paolo has made good—on paper, at least."

"Who were these mysterious masterminds who planned the bank robbery?" Sydney asked, leaning forward eagerly in his chair. "You hinted at ties to the British establishment."

"The bank robbery was a joint venture between the Amassi gang and two budding politicians, one of whom holds a position in our current government, and the other heads one of our intelligence agencies." Jocelyn's face contorted, and he looked from side to side as though his enemies would leap out the dining room's walls. "Now, do you see why I have to be careful?"

I caught Sidney's eye. Over the last few months, we'd grown good at reading one another's thoughts. Right now, he mirrored my skepticism. I believed the part about the Moretti twins' involvement in the bank robbery. I bought the idea that Paolo had set up his drug-import business using his share of the proceeds. But a government-level conspiracy? That part read like a plot twist in one of Lucky's mysteries. It was time to steer the conversation back to finding my brother.

"Thanks for sharing, Jocelyn." I tried to keep my voice neutral and not betray my doubt in the veracity of his account. "I'm so sorry about your dad."

Jocelyn contemplated his ragged, bitten nails. "It was a long time ago, but some wounds never heal."

"Regarding my brother, we can guess Paolo Moretti is behind his kidnapping. The question is, how do we find him l before the deadline? I'm not optimistic that we'll scrabble together fifty thousand euros in cash, so we need to rescue Del."

"You won't like this suggestion, Angel," Sidney said, "but maybe we should consider roping in Chief Inspector Colombo. We're in Italy alone, with no backup from the Omega Group. We don't even have stun guns, let alone proper weapons. Even if we find

Del, how are we going to get him away from his kidnappers? They're bound to be armed."

"I can help with that." Jocelyn pushed back his chair and pulled up his robes, revealing an alarming arsenal strapped to his body.

Sidney and I leaped to our feet with a collective gasp.

"What in the world, Jocelyn?" Sidney demanded. "Do you have a license for any of those firearms?"

His cousin slid two Glocks out of their holsters and handed them to us. "No, and nor do you. I work on the assumption that it's better to get my knuckles rapped for illegal possession of a firearm than to get killed because I'm the only idiot with no means to defend himself."

I took a Glock and turned to Sidney. "He's right, you know. We're on our own. Chief Inspector Colombo lives in Monterosso. Maybe he's in Paolo Moretti's pay."

"If he is, it'd explain why he's so determined to pin Lucky's murder on me," Jocelyn interjected. "I'm not sure if Paolo Moretti knows I'm working on a book about the robbery. He may even know my father was one of its victims. He definitely won't want me digging into his past in case it causes him problems in the present. Paolo did time for the robbery, yes, but if it transpires that he received any of the stolen money, that's a whole new case to answer."

I slid back into my seat and released a long breath. "You think *you* were the intended victim?"

"That possibility didn't occur to you, Ms. Private Detective?" He scoffed. "I'd have thought it was obvious. What better way to nix my story than to murder me? Dead men don't write books."

"It crossed my mind, yes, but it seems unlikely that Paolo dispatched an assassin to get rid of you, and Lucky was killed in a case of mistaken identity. All day we've had people telling us how well-known Lucky is in Cinque Terre. Do you expect us to believe that Paolo Moretti—a man you say has evaded prosecution for decades—hired an assassin so stupid he murdered the wrong man?"

Sidney stared at his Glock before slipping it into his jacket pocket. "I agree with Angel. It doesn't add up. Beyond the dark hair, you and Lucky didn't look alike. We still don't know what Lucky was doing at the villa when he wasn't due back in Monterosso until April. Couldn't his sudden presence in Italy be connected to his murder? Maybe his plot line for his next book upset the wrong people."

Jocelyn slammed his fists on the table, making our dinner plates dance. "Lucky wrote fiction, not true crime exposés. Who'd want to kill an author for making up a story that may or may not have some elements of fact? My book is a direct attack on Paolo and everyone else involved in masterminding that bank robbery. Why don't you believe I'm the intended victim?"

"I'm willing to consider the possibility," I said, "but if you want our help to clear you of the suspicion of Lucky's murder, Sidney and I will have to explore all options, including Lucky being the intended victim."

Sidney swallowed his last forkful of *trofie al pesto*. "Paolo Moretti is the common denominator in the kidnapping and the murder. I suggest Angel and I stick to our original plan of finding her brother before the ransom is due to be delivered."

Jocelyn quirked an eyebrow. "Ever heard the phrase, looking for a needle in a haystack? Where do you think Paolo is keeping Del hostage?"

I related my brother's text messages and my theory that he might be in one of the abandoned buildings in the hills of Cinque Terre. "That's why we're planning to hike the Vernazza-Corniglia trail tomorrow, and then take a boat out to see if we can spot any suspicious activity at sea."

This amused Jocelyn. "There's always suspicious activity at sea. Do you even know what Paolo's fishing boat looks like?"

Sidney looked at me and grinned. "No. Which is why we're hoping you'll take us out on your boat."

"Provided that fool Colombo hasn't arrested me in the meantime, I'm having lunch with Gianni's son tomorrow. Why don't we meet outside the restaurant at two? Then I'll drive us back to Monterosso, and we can pick up the *Mary Celeste*."

I coughed back a laugh, not daring to look at

Sidney for fear of setting off a fit of giggles. Trust Jocelyn to name his boat after the ghost ship that had spawned countless conspiracy theories and a fictional namesake, the *Marie Celeste*, featured in a story penned by Arthur Conan Doyle.

Our host checked the wine bottle and refilled our glasses. "Do you want dessert before I get the bill? I can drive you back to Monterosso when we're done here."

"I'm too stuffed to think about dessert," I admitted, "something I never say. Gianni's food is delicious."

"I'm with Angel," Sidney said. "This afternoon, I discovered the pure ecstasy that is Arturo's gelato. If they're still open when we get back to Monterosso, I'm having another scoop."

After Jocelyn paid for our meal, and we'd all offered profuse thanks to Gianni and his cooks, we drove back to Monterosso in Jocelyn's bumblebee yellow Piaggio Ape. I was not-so-secretly thrilled at the prospect of riding in one of the three-wheeled scooter vans beloved by Italians. While I rode shotgun with Jocelyn at the wheel, Sidney and Bernice piled into the back. Having snoozed through our dinner, the dog was delighted to be on the move. She happy-howled all the way back to town.

Our hotel had no guest parking, so Jocelyn drove to the beachside parking lot where I'd left the rental car. When we got out of the van, there was a commotion on the beach, complete with blue flashing lights. Bernice strained at her leash, eager to investigate. I forced her over to my car, where I grabbed the rest of my stuff out of the boot. The dog wouldn't stop making a fuss.

I looked at Sidney and shrugged. "We need to take her out before bed, in any case. We can stroll by the beach on our way to Arturo's."

"Not I," Jocelyn said with a shudder. "I have no desire to rub shoulders with the police—they might decide to arrest me. I'm heading back to the hotel."

"Want me to bring you back a cone?" Sidney asked. "Arturo's gelato is amazing."

"No, thanks." Jocelyn wrinkled his nose. "Arturo only has two vegan options. I prefer the sorbet parlor in the old town."

After we parted ways with Sidney's cousin, we took Bernice down to the beach. Sensing adventure, the dog made a beeline for the cluster of people huddled by the water's edge.

Two police officers were attempting to stem the tide of curious onlookers, but with little success.

I nudged Sidney. "Colombo's standing next to the ambulance, taking to the paramedics. Did someone have an accident at sea?"

Sidney was considerably taller than me and had a better view. He looked down at me, his face grim. "They've dragged a body out of the water."

That horrible coil of panic unfurled again, turning my feet to cement. "Male or female? Young or old?"

He strained to get a better look. "A man, I'd say.

Not sure about his age. Thirties? Forties? He's face down on the sand, but they're turning him over now."

Dropping Bernice's leash, I forced my feet into motion, slow and staggering at first, then gathering speed.

"Angel, wait up."

I ignored Sidney and kept moving, dragging myself over the sand. Had Dani's hunch been right all along? Had Moretti held my brother captive on a boat? And if Moretti was so fickle as to double the ransom demand in less than twenty-four hours, had he changed his mind about the money and killed Del instead?

Paying no heed to the warning shout of the police officers, I hurtled toward the prone figure on the sand. I reached the dead man just as the paramedics placed him on his back and wiped the seaweed from his face.

My breath caught in a silent scream.

For the second time since my arrival in Monterosso, I was faced with a pair of blank, staring eyes. And, once again, those eyes didn't belong to my brother.

Lifeless on the sand, an unnatural dent caving in the side of his head, lay Del's friend Marco.

## 19

*I* have no memory of crying out. Exhaustion accumulated over several sleepless nights crashed over me, tsunami-style. One moment, I was wedged in the wet sand, transfixed by Marco's dead face. The next, Sidney was at my side, pulling me back from the body. With the benefit of hindsight, my reaction was a heady mixture of relief that the dead man wasn't Del and terror that my brother would be the next to die.

Sidney hauled me away from my brother's dead friend and took me in his arms. Besides being the world's most reluctant hugger, I rarely cry. Tonight, I emulated a heroine in an 80s romance novel, sagging against his surprisingly muscular chest and sobbing into his shirt. Bernice sidled up to me, whining with concern, and pressed herself against my legs.

Unlike an 80s romance heroine, I don't cry

delicately. Within seconds of the onset of my crying jag, I was a blubbering, snorting mess.

Sidney's shirt bore the brunt of the damage, but he was unfazed. He stroked back my unruly curls. "I'm so sorry, Angel. Is it Del?"

"No. It's his friend, Marco—the guy I spoke to yesterday." I pulled back from our embrace, found a tissue in my pocket, and honked. "But you see what this means? The threats to kill him are genuine. Del's a dead man if we don't find the ransom money before tomorrow night."

"Not if we find him first." He handed me a fresh tissue. "The police are right here. Maybe it's time to confide in them about your brother."

Looming out of the darkness like a villain in a bad horror movie, Chief Inspector Colombo materialized by my side. "What's that you say?" He demanded in English. "What about your brother?"

I whipped around and came face-to-face with the glowering inspector. On instinct, I grabbed hold of Bernice, staving off another licking frenzy.

Colombo looked even grumpier than when we'd last met, and his beige raincoat had descended from rumpled to bedraggled. "The dead man was my brother's friend," I said simply. "Seeing him like this came as a shock."

"You seem to be a dead body magnet, Ms. Doyle," Colombo growled, getting up in my face, his entire manner aggressive and accusatory. "Do you make a habit of falling over corpses?"

The honest answer would be yes, but I had zero intention of supplying the man with ammunition he could use to keep me at the police station for a second night. To have any chance of finding my brother before the kidnappers' deadline, I had to remain free to move around Cinque Terre.

As it happened, a shout from one of Colombo's junior officers spared me from making a response. The second policeman pointed at an object on the sand beside the body.

With a snarl, Colombo stood back, glaring at me. "I told you to stay put. I hear you've been all over Cinque Terre today."

"I'm on holiday," I replied tartly. "Of course, I want to see the sights. I surrendered my ID, as requested, and I agreed to stay in the area. I haven't set foot outside the national park."

He grunted. "I'd rather you stayed in Monterosso."

"Rather away," I snapped. "I'm under no obligation to hole up in my hotel room simply because you can't solve a case. As a courtesy, I'm informing you I intend to hike the Vernazza-Corniglia trail tomorrow morning, followed by a boat trip in the afternoon. All still within the Cinque Terre area."

"Sir?" the junior officer called again. "You really need to see this."

Colombo swore under his breath. "I'm keeping my

eye on you, Ms. Doyle." He swung around to confront Sidney. "And on your cousin. I don't trust any of you."

He stomped off, kicking up sand, and left us straining to see what his colleague had discovered.

"It looks like a wallet," Sidney said, using his superior height to peer over the crowd.

I folded my arms across my chest and fired a death ray glance at Colombo's hunched back. "Do you still think I should confide in that man?"

"No, especially not with how he's greeting the new arrival on the scene."

"What new arrival?" I strained to get a look and my stomach went into a freefall when I saw Colombo's new chum.

Paolo Moretti stood next to the police officer, who'd called over to Colombo. He shook hands with the chief inspector, greeting him like a long-lost friend. Colombo had his back to us, so we couldn't read his expression. But he pumped hands with Moretti, and they talked for a while, looking down at the dead man on the sand.

"I've seen enough." I took Bernice's leash, and we headed back up to the street.

"Do you still want to stop for gelato?" Sidney asked when we neared Arturo's gelateria. "If not, I'll just run in and get a cone for me."

I pushed back a tangle of hair and rubbed my aching eyes. "Actually, comfort food sounds good."

Bernice trotted into Arturo's and zoomed over to

the table Sidney and I had occupied earlier. She sat beside the table, panting.

"Good girl, but we're not staying." I nodded to Barbie, who was cleaning the coffee machine. "Sidney mentioned you had white chocolate gelato. I'd like a scoop in a cone, please."

"Sure thing." Barbie grinned at Sidney, who was openly drooling at the selection. "And what will you have? One of each?"

Leaving them to sort the ice cream order, I wandered over to the only occupied table.

Ken sat with an older woman I didn't recognize, drinking freshly squeezed lemonade. His cornflower blue trousers and red wrap-around shirt made him look like a cross between a Buddhist monk and a dude-bro marketer. His companion was an elegant fifty-something with sleek black hair and full lips painted a peachy pink.

In a faintly mocking tone, Ken made the introductions. "Maria, this is Jimmy's sister, Kimmy. Kimmy, Maria also lives at Villa Margherita."

Ah, Maria Bianchi from apartment four. "Nice to meet you, Maria." I gestured toward Sidney. "That's Jocelyn's cousin, Sidney."

Sidney waved a cheery greeting and returned to the crucial of matter of which gelato flavors he'd order for tonight's fix.

The introductions over, Ken's smug smirk slid back

into place. "I saw you get arrested last night. The police let you go?"

"Shockingly, yes." I treated him to a honeyed smile. "Jocelyn, too. Perhaps they'll arrest *you* next."

His smug smirk proved as durable as flaky meringue. "What? Why? *I* had nothing to do with the murder."

Happy to let him flounder, I focused on Maria. "Have the police discovered anything new?"

Her peachy lips flattened. "Not as far as I know. You've heard about the blood in the basement?"

"I have, yeah. So that's where Lucky was killed?"

"I don't know," Maria replied. "There's a rumor doing the rounds that Lucky's body was stored in the basement shortly after his death, but he wasn't actually killed there."

"Why don't the police believe he died in the basement?"

"Not enough blood, apparently," Ken added, toying with his lemonade glass.

"Don't forget Saul's tent is missing," Barbie called from behind the gelato counter. "The police think Lucky was killed on top of the tent, and then the killer got rid of it. That would account for the lack of blood on the ground."

Maria shuddered. "It's all so horrible. And to think I might have heard the murderer..."

I pounced on this revelation. "When? Where?"

"When I was coming upstairs to Saul and

Riccardo's apartment, I heard the lift. I didn't see who was using it, though."

"What time was this?"

"Around six-twenty? I can't be precise. I was concentrating on not dropping the tray of lasagne I'd made for the party." Maria huddled into her cashmere shawl. "This business has shaken me. It's terrible to think a killer is on the loose. I was so relieved to meet Ken on the train. He's going to walk Barbie and me back to the villa."

"Do you have any idea who'd want Lucky dead?" I asked. "I understand he wasn't a popular bloke, but who'd want to kill him?"

"I wouldn't describe Lucky as unpopular," Maria said, to my surprise. "He was one of those larger-than-life characters who divide opinion. His murder has everyone focusing on why he was killed, but many people loved having him in Monterosso. Lucky was a big spender, and his books brought attention to the region."

"Yet someone hated him enough to stick a poker in his back," I countered. "Can you think of a reason for Lucky to show up at Villa Margherita out of the blue at this time of year?"

"I'm stumped," Ken said. "Lucky hated the cold. To you and me, the weather in Monterosso in November is pretty mild, but Lucky spent the winter months at his condo in Miami."

Armed with two cones—one single-scoop, the other

ginormous—Sidney appeared at my side. "Here you go. Welcome to tastebud heaven."

I took the cone, and we said our goodbyes. Back out on the street, I recounted the conversation to Sidney while Bernice wandered ahead, sniffing the pavement.

"You really don't like Ken, do you?" Sidney chuckled. "I could tell just by observing your body language. You stood ram-rod straight and defensive."

"Ken gives me the creeps." I wrinkled my nose. "I wish Colombo would arrest him."

"Colombo might just do that. Barbie was telling me that Saul and Riccardo are currently at the police station, answering questions about their missing tent. At this rate, Colombo will have everyone at the Villa Margherita languishing in an interrogation room."

We finished our gelato on the way back to the hotel. Sidney hadn't exaggerated. My white chocolate gelato was the best I'd ever tasted. Sidney was effusive about all his flavors and vowed to go back to try more.

Sidney had booked me a room next to his and Jocelyn's. When we reached our doors, Bernice went wild. She leaped at Sidney's door, barking, growling, and generally freaking out.

Perplexed, Sidney and I and stared at one another.

"What's this about?" he asked. "Is she reacting to Jocelyn's scent?"

"I'm afraid I don't speak dog." A horrible thought descended. "You don't think—?"

Sidney slid his keycard into the slot and barged

ZARA KEANE

into the room. Bernice charged past him, barking and snarling. A familiar feline yowling added to the cacophony.

Jocelyn and his six cats sat on the beds, all in a state of anxiety. "Get that dog out of here," Jocelyn cried. "I don't want her anywhere near my babies."

I grabbed Bernice and hauled her out into the hall.

Sidney ran a hand through his hair. "What in the world, Jocelyn? Why did you bring the cats here? This is my room, too."

"Dani called," Jocelyn said sulkily. "She demanded I take them back. Said it was too much work. What else could I do? I can't move back into my apartment until tomorrow evening."

"Right." Sidney slowly exhaled. "I'll grab my stuff and move next door with Angel. I can deal with one cat, but six at once? No way."

"Unbelievable," Sidney muttered when we were safely in my room, and Bernice was distracted with a toy. "I was doing him a favor by letting him stay in my room. It wasn't an open invitation to have a cat orgy."

"No worries. Bernice and I don't mind having a boy in our room."

Sidney padded over to his suitcase and rubbed his jaw. "This boy needs a shower and a shave. I'm still sticky after our hike."

"While you shower, I'll check in with Dani." My gaze shifted from my laptop to my phone, and my fingers turned to ice. "And I should probably return Dad's call."

When Sidney disappeared into the bathroom, I checked my phone messages. There was one from Dani, sent an hour ago. She'd persuaded her uncle to give her fifteen thousand euros to put toward the ransom. She ended the message by saying she was on her way to bed, but that I should call her if I had any news.

And there was another missed call from Dad.

I poured a glass of sparkling water and took a long drink. I wasn't ready to talk to my father. His rejection still stung, even after all this time. But Del was in serious danger. Marco's death had hammered home the extent of his peril. If Dad could help, either with information or money, I needed to swallow my pride and make that call.

Dad answered on the first ring. "Angel?"

ad's familiar gravelly voice elicited all the feels. Noel Doyle had lived in London for nearly thirty years, but he'd never lost his County Clare accent.

"Yeah, it's me. What's up?" *What's up?* We hadn't spoken in two years. Couldn't I think of anything more profound to say to the man?

My father got straight to the point. "I had a call from a complete stranger today. Some Italian fella calling himself Locatelli. He had some cock and bull story about Del being held for ransom and you running around Italy looking for him. What the actual—?"

Yes, gentle reader, I inherited my bluntness from my dad. "It's true," I said, and gave him a concise overview of everything that had occurred since I received Del's first text message.

When I'd finished, my father grunted, a sound that

conveyed frustration and disbelief. "We can't name names on the phone, but you know who she is, right?"

"I do. Not a family I want to mess with."

"No more do I," my father muttered. "This is a bad business. Del's always been a hopeless case, but this latest stunt is the limit. Where do they expect me to find fifty grand by tomorrow? Up my—?"

"Dad, I get the picture. Dani—that's the name she's using in Monterosso—says her uncle can give her fifteen thousand by tomorrow. Did he mention that to you?"

"Yeah. The story stinks worse than week-old fish. Are you sure this isn't a scheme cooked up by Del and lady friend?"

"I considered that possibility, but Dani's fear is the real deal. And tonight's events cemented my certainty." I filled him in on Marco's death and elaborated upon my theory that Paolo Moretti was holding Del hostage because Del had accidentally destroyed a shipment of drugs.

When I finished, Dad remained ominously silent for several elongated seconds. "This Paolo Moretti was part of the Amassi bank robbery?"

"Yeah. He served fifteen years and then moved back to Monterosso, presumably with his share of the proceeds."

"The Amassis were long before my time," my father said. "I can ask around for details about the Moretti twins. Jimmy might know."

ZARA KEANE

Jimmy the Rat, my godfather and Dad's longtime bestie, had a past more colorful than a preschooler's artwork. Had Del picked his Italian alias after Jimmy? It wouldn't surprise me. My brother didn't exactly burst with imagination.

"Yeah, please do. You can contact me at this number if you find anything."

That noncommittal grunt again. "Send me your bank details, and I'll arrange the transfer. I want you to handle the money, not your brother or his girlfriend."

"Fair enough. I can't say I blame you."

A pause, a throat-clearing. "I hear you're living in Nice with Desirée. How is your mother?"

"Sending waves of anger across the Med in my direction. And we're not living together. She's letting me stay at her house in Antibes." I didn't add that this arrangement was most likely past tense.

"I hope your new life works out for you, Angel." His words were low, indistinct. If I didn't know Dad better, I'd suspect he was crying. "I'd better go. Things to do, you know?"

A stab of disappointment popped the balloon of hope I hadn't noticed inflating. "Okay, then. I...guess I'll hear from you."

He rang off abruptly, leaving me listening to the beep-beep chorus. Dad hadn't suggested meeting for a meaningful catch-up. He'd made no expressions of regret over ignoring me for two whole years. But had I truly expected any other reaction from the man? Dad

218

was an affectionate father when his kids were in his good books. Equally, he had no qualms about cutting us off if we displeased him.

I'd always known this side of my father existed—he'd had frequent dustups with my brothers over the years. Yet he'd never cut me dead until I informed on his boss's son. And it had devastated me.

In one fluid movement, I leaped off my bed, tossing my phone onto my nightstand. Moping was a luxury I couldn't afford. I stalked to my suitcase, retrieved my laptop, and fired up my search engine of choice. Sidney and I had a busy schedule tomorrow, and I needed to know more about the residents of Villa Margherita.

When Sidney emerged from the shower, clad in PJs and towel-drying his hair, I was wholly absorbed in my task.

He laughed when he saw me sitting cross-legged on my bed, frowning at my laptop. "Let me guess—you're internet stalking everyone we spoke to today."

"Not quite everyone. I'm confining my efforts to the residents of Villa Margherita. Why don't you grab your laptop and practice those internet Ninja skills I've been teaching you?"

"A classic Angel and Sidney divide-and-conquer moment." He grabbed his laptop and flopped onto the bed beside me. "How far have you gotten?"

"I've already covered Maria Bianchi and the party hosts, Saul and Riccardo."

"Anything stand out?"

"Apart from how unlikely they all seem to be cold-blooded killers? No. Saul and Riccardo run a photography business. They're active on social media, but mostly for work, and they have a company website. Maria Bianchi is a retired civil servant. According to her social media profiles, she enjoys gardening and playing canasta." I stretched my neck from side to side, feeling the burn. "Why don't you tackle Barbie while I dig the dirt on Ken and the Carrington sisters?"

Sidney made a mock salute. "Yes, ma'am." He poured himself a glass of sparkling water, cracked his knuckles, and got to work.

Thirty minutes and many notes later, I was still trawling through Ken's various past businesses, none of which had lasted, including a luxury yoga retreat center that went bust two years ago. I yawned and stretched. "Find anything interesting on the *Surfer Bay* alien abductee?"

"Interesting, yes. Relevant? The jury's still out." He bounced on the bed, an excited gleam in his eyes. "Barbie attended a weight loss clinic after she left *Surfer Bay* and moved to L.A. in a bid to break into Hollywood."

"Given that she's now slinging gelato in Monterosso, I take it her plans didn't work out. Any dirt?"

"Not that I can find," Sidney said with a note of regret. "She made a couple of TV pilots, but neither series was picked up. Eventually, her American agent dropped her, and she moved back to Australia."

"Ouch," I said, wincing. "That's rough."

"As a fellow former actor who spent more time resting than working, I sympathize. Fan message boards think Barbie's weight loss was a mistake. Part of her charm when she appeared in *Surfer Bay* was her size. She was curvier than all the other bikini-clad actresses in the show, and this made her relatable."

"Do the fan boards know how she hooked up with Ken?" I asked, genuinely intrigued. "Apart from me not liking the dude, he seems an unlikely choice for Barbie. There's quite an age gap."

"Barbie and Ken met when she attended a yoga retreat at a wellness center Ken ran on an island in the Great Barrier Reef. They fell for one another and moved to Italy for a fresh start."

"Yes, the wellness center." I jabbed a finger at my notepad. "That was one of the many businesses Ken has run over the years—before they went bust."

"Yikes. Any sign of illicit dealings?"

"A former employer had Ken investigated for embezzlement, but the case was dropped due to lack of hard evidence." I beamed at Sidney. "And—drumroll—Ken had a falling out with Lucky Lucchese over money. Apparently, the first summer Ken lived in Monterosso, he convinced Lucky to invest in his tech startup—something to do with developing an app for tourists visiting Cinque Terre. Like Ken's previous businesses, the company crashed on take-off. I knew that guy was dodgy."

Sidney closed his laptop and shuffled across the twin beds to sit beside me. "Where did you find this information?"

"Notes from a local council meeting. Apparently, Lucky wasn't the only person Ken fleeced." I angled my computer screen so that Sidney could read the minutes. I was confident he'd understand them—Sidney's Italian was better than mine.

After perusing the notes, he sat back and looked at me. "Do you think Ken is simply a lousy businessman or deliberately committing fraud?"

"Dunno. But I'd run from any investment opportunity he pitched me." I pointed at his laptop screen. "Any luck finding a link between Barbie and Lucky Lucchese?"

"Absolutely nothing. Beyond Barbie's professional woes, her digital footprint is a blank. What did you discover about the Carringtons?"

My fingers flew over my keyboard. "I'm just checking now. I fell down a rabbit hole of hating on Ken. Okay, here we go, easy-peasy. Heather Carrington is forty years old and works part time for a charity devoted to helping children with physical disabilities. Her sister, Lucy, is thirty-eight and works as a pediatrician in a private practice in London. In their social media profiles, they describe themselves as single, and the home address listed for both sisters in the phone book is identical."

Sidney whistled in appreciation. "You're good. You found all of that out in just a few clicks?"

"I also saved photos of each of our suspects in case we need to show them to people tomorrow."

I scrolled through various search results, scanning the headings. Heather didn't generate many hits, but Lucy was referenced in medical journals and as a speaker at conferences. I clicked to open the second page of the search results.

And hit gold.

I sucked in a breath in stages, barely believing what I was reading. "Sidney, I have something."

He slid closer to me, so close our thighs touched. "What have you found?"

Weirdly aware of the heat of his leg next to mine, I gave myself a mental shaking. *Focus, Angel.* "The Carringtons' father was an eminent Harley Street plastic surgeon. When the girls were little, suspected burglars broke into his practice after closing and killed him. Five-year-old Heather was with her father at the time and was badly wounded in the attack."

Sidney skimmed the account over my shoulder. "Horrendous, but I don't see the relevance to Lucky's murder."

My heart quickened in building excitement. "Neither do I. At least, not yet. But there might be a link to Paolo Moretti."

"What link? What am I missing?"

I jabbed a thumb at my laptop screen. "The significance of *when* the burglary took place. Heather was five. Now she's forty. This went down *thirty-five* years ago, the same year Paolo and his twin brother helped the Amassi gang commit one of the biggest bank robberies in recent history."

Sidney leaned over and read the article more thoroughly. "It's a bit of a stretch, Angel. Why would Paolo rob a plastic surgeon's office?"

I input another search. "See this newspaper report? The bank robbery took place on the 5th of April. Dr. Carrington died on the 30th of June. Same year, just a few weeks apart."

"Wasn't Paolo locked up by then?" Sidney countered. "I understood from Jocelyn that Paolo was arrested at the scene of the bank robbery. There wouldn't have been time for the case to come to trial, but I can't image Paolo was given bail."

I raised my palms. "Dude, I don't know. All I'm saying is it's a coincidence. I'd like to know more about Dr. Carrington's death."

Sidney slid off the bed and fetched his backpack. Armed with a notebook and a pen, he sat opposite me, pen poised. "Let's make a list of our suspects and theories, starting with the people we don't want to be guilty. Why would my cousin kill Lucky?"

I bounced into my role. "Jocelyn is paranoia personified. He was worried that Lucky was stealing his story. If Lucky published a novel featuring a plot similar to Joceyln's allegations against Paolo Moretti, no one would take Jocelyn's account seriously. Everyone would assume your cousin was cashing in on Lucky's reputation. And don't forget that Jocelyn is responsible for the villa's surveillance cameras being switched off."

"All valid points." Sidney scribbled in his notebook. "Continuing to rip off our personal bandages, I'll take your brother. What if Del killed Lucky while high on drugs? He came back to Villa Margherita after a night of debauchery and was shocked to discover Lucky on the premises. For reasons I haven't yet figured out, they got into a fight, and Del stabbed Lucky with a poker. Then he stashed the corpse in the basement and raided Riccardo's costume box for a disguise."

"And subsequently lured me to Italy, faked his own kidnapping, and demanded a ransom sufficient for him and Dani to abscond to another country?" I screwed up my nose. "I'm not digging this theory. Del's not the cleverest of cats, but even he knows fifty thousand euros isn't enough for two adults and a baby to pull a Houdini."

Sidney threw up his arms. "So my story has more holes than Swiss cheese. All I'm saying is we can't dismiss Del as a suspect just because he's your brother."

I snatched his notebook and pen. "We've covered

our family members. What about the others? Did Maria Bianchi lose money to Lucky during a game of canasta?"

"Canasta isn't considered a gambling game. My grandmother is a keen bridge and canasta player. Both games depend on a high degree of skill, not luck."

"Fine," I said. "Could she have had an affair with Lucky that ended badly? He had a reputation as a womanizer."

"The villa is a hive of gossip, yet no one's mentioned a liaison between Maria and Lucky." Sidney grimaced. "We'll have to admit defeat and mark Maria as an unlikely murder suspect. What about Saul and Riccardo? Maybe Lucky promised to feature their photography business in *Murdered in Monterosso*, but reneged on the deal."

"That's a decent theory," I said, making a note.

"What about the Carrington sisters?" Sidney asked. "Can we bump them off the shortlist for Lucky's murder? Even if my hunch about the fatal burglary is correct, the tentative link is with Paolo Moretti, not Lucky Lucchese."

"With great reluctance, I agree." I stared gloomily at our notes, or lack thereof. "That leaves Jocelyn and Del as our prime suspects."

Sidney prised the notebook from my fingers. "We're not going to find answers tonight. Get some sleep. We have a trail to hike tomorrow, not to mention a kidnapper to catch."

21

The next morning, Sidney and I rose early, grabbed a quick breakfast at the hotel restaurant, and caught the train from Monterosso to Vernazza. The Glock Jocelyn had given me felt comfortable in my jacket pocket. I wasn't used to carrying a pistol, let alone using one, and I'd have some serious explaining to do if I had to use it today. However, I'd rather risk getting into trouble with the cops than losing my life.

Bernice was delighted to hang out with us again. Sidney had developed a bond with her. And despite my lack of experience with dogs, I had to admit I was fond of Bernice and her shaggy shenanigans. How diligent was Del about bringing her for regular walks? I'd only been in the dog's company for a couple of days, yet it was obvious how well-behaved she was once she got sufficient exercise. Was her reputation for being wild simply a lack of physical stimulation?

I tried calling Dani when we were on the train but kept getting her voicemail. Her lack of responsiveness made me uneasy. "Still no reply," I said to Sidney, slipping the phone back into my pocket. "I hope she's okay."

His expression was grim. "So do I. The last thing we need today is her going into labor."

"That's exactly what I'm worried about. If Dani's busy giving birth, how will we access her uncle's contribution to the ransom fund in time for tonight's deadline?"

Sidney got out his phone. "I'll call Jocelyn and ask him to drop by her apartment to check on her. He mentioned swinging by the villa this morning to collect kitty litter from his basement stash."

We exited the train at Vernazza and made our way to the start of the Vernazza-Corniglia hiking trail. With the notable exception of the brutal stone steps, I'd enjoyed yesterday's hike, and the views had more than made up for my initial discomfort. In contrast, today's hiking trail was a pure pleasure from start to finish. The incline was moderate, and the path clung gloriously to the cliff edge, providing us with unparalleled sea views the entire way. The weather was once again excellent for November, and we took plenty of photos while keeping our eyes peeled for potential kidnappers' lairs.

At the halfway point of the trail, we stumbled upon a hilarious incongruity. Out of the ether sprung a stone edifice housing a lemonade stand. The menu listed lemonade in various degrees of sweetness, plus several fortified offerings. I opted for a medium-sweet, non-alcoholic lemonade. Sidney went all in and ordered an extra sour with double vodka shots.

We were the only customers at the lemonade joint, but I imagined the place was packed during the summer. While Sidney and I waited for our order, we watched a waiter arrange trays of beverages for a photography shoot. I only half-listened to their conversation until I heard the name Riccardo. Squeezing Sidney's arm, I detached myself from the bar and approached the men.

"Sorry to interrupt," I said in Italian, "but is one of you Riccardo Ventimiglia from Villa Margherita?"

The shorter of the two—a fair-haired man of about forty—whipped around at the mention of his name. "That's right." He squinted at me dubiously. "Have we met?"

"No." I extended a hand. "I'm Jimmy's sister. I came to visit him and Dani and wound up a murder suspect. What a way to spend a holiday."

Riccardo's smile was uncertain. "Yeah, I heard you had to go to the police station."

"Not my idea of a fun first day in Italy."

The tension in his face ebbed. "They questioned my husband and I yesterday. The police believe the

ZARA KEANE

murderer used our tent to mop up the blood. It took us five hours to convince them we had nothing to do with Lucky's death. We barely knew the guy."

"I hadn't even met him." I smiled at the waiter, who hovered with a fresh tray of drinks for Riccardo to photograph. "Apologies for interrupting your work. This has all been so traumatic."

"Tell me about it," the waiter said, shaking his head. "And now we have that waiter murdered on the beach. What is the place coming to? Cinque Terre is a peaceful place, yet we've had two suspicious deaths."

"We don't know that Marco was murdered," Riccardo said, shooting me a sidelong glance. "He might have hit his head in an accident. We won't know more until the inquest."

"I saw Chief Inspector Colombo on the beach last night when Marco's body was found. I suppose that means he's in charge of both investigations. What sort of man is he? Do you think he's competent?"

The waiter shifted his weight from one foot to the other, clearly uncomfortable with my line of questioning, but Riccardo simply shrugged. "Hard to say. I see Colombo and his family around the town, but I don't know them well. They live in a very nice villa with a pool, about ten minutes higher in the hills than Villa Margherita."

"Reading between the lines, you wonder how Colombo can afford such a house on a police salary." I winked at Riccardo. "Don't look so shocked. I'm good at picking up hints."

"Oy!" Sidney shouted from the counter. "Stop gossiping and start walking. Our order is ready."

"Nice talking to you, Riccardo. Maybe I'll see you at the villa."

Riccardo looked less than enthused at the idea of a second encounter with his neighbor's nosy sister. I couldn't blame him. I'd have given me a wide berth, too. Generally, I preferred to avoid the direct attack when questioning suspects, but today, I was short on time.

The second half of our hike was uneventful. Plenty of photo ops, but no obvious candidates for a kidnapper's hideout.

By the time we descended the rope-lined path into Corniglia, my mood was despondent. Were we wasting our time? And had I made a mistake by refusing to go to the police?

The memory of Paolo Moretti's hand in Chief Inspector Colombo's snapped me out of my doldrums. "Want to do a repeat of yesterday?" I asked Sidney.

"Sure, but why don't I take Bernice this time?" He checked his watch. "Want to meet back here in an hour? That'll give us enough time to talk to people before we need to meet Jocelyn at Monterosso's harbor."

As I'd suspected, Corniglia in daylight was even more beautiful than at night. I tore my gaze away from the gorgeous colored buildings and concentrated on the people. My attempts at gleaning information from the locals yielded underwhelming results. Some had liked Lucky, some couldn't stand him, and no one wanted to discuss Paolo Moretti with a stranger.

After a fruitless hour of badgering the natives, I trudged back to meet Sidney and Bernice. Feeling stressed, and oddly bereft, I wasn't paying attention to my surroundings. I hadn't gone five paces when I careened into a woman carrying a pile of rugs. She lost hold of her wares, and they landed on the cobblestones.

Muttering embarrassed apologies, I helped her to pick up her stock. When my fingers registered the texture of what I was holding, soft and silky, with a smooth underside, I took a closer look. I was holding a good quality white sheepskin rug, similar to the one on which the late Lucky Lucchese had been lying when Sidney and I had found him in Jocelyn's apartment.

## 22

My heart quickened a beat, a theory crystallizing. Jocelyn had been adamant that the sheepskin rug didn't belong to him. If so, it must have come from either the basement or from one of the other apartments at Villa Margherita. Whoever had moved Lucky's body had probably grabbed the rug at the last minute, for reasons I couldn't yet figure out. Were they assuaging a guilty conscience by laying the body on a soft rug instead of dumping it on stone tiles? And if they swiped the rug from the basement or an apartment, would they seek to replace it before its owner noticed it was missing?

My theory was more raw than half-baked, but I was low on time and high on desperation. I confronted the irritated shop owner. "Do you sell many of these sheepskin rugs? Have you sold any recently?"

Scenting a sale, the woman's attitude toward me

softened. "They're very popular, both the pure white version and the white-beige variety. Come into my shop, and I can offer you an excellent deal."

Resigned to the fact that information about her customer list was going to cost me, I followed the shop's owner into her lair.

After an awkward negotiation, I settled on the smallest and least expensive of her rugs. To my horror, this crime against home decor set me back close to two hundred euros. I added it to my mental expense list and vowed to bill my brother the instant I rescued his sorry backside.

I made a show of oohing and aahing over my purchase. "I'm staying at Villa Margherita in Monterosso. When I saw a rug similar to the one I showed you outside, I knew I had to have one. Do you know Villa Margherita? It's a gorgeous house up in the hills."

The woman cocked her head to the side and screwed up her eyes in contemplation. "The name sounds familiar, but there are so many fancy villas in Cinque Terre."

"Villa Margherita is all over the news." I lowered my voice to a conspiratorial whisper. "It's where the author Lucky Lucchese was murdered."

The shop owner's hand flew to her mouth in a comically overdramatic gesture. "Seriously? Do you have any insider info?"

"Not really," I lied, trying to recall what I'd seen

reported in the local paper this morning. I opted for a nugget of information that would be widely known shortly, even if it wasn't already common knowledge. "Apparently, Lucky's body was moved after death. The police aren't sure where he was killed."

My listener gasped with pleasure and pumped me for more details. I indulged her curiosity with a couple of harmless tidbits and then steered the conversation back to the sheepskin rugs. "Can you tell me if you sold any of the medium-sized pure white rugs in the last couple of days? Perhaps to one of these people?" I slipped my phone out of my pocket and showed her photos of the villa residents that I'd saved last night.

I flipped through the pictures one by one. The shop owner shook her head each time and encouraged me to keep swiping. When I reached the photo of Lucy Carrington, she grew excited. "That English lady. I recognize her."

"You do? Did she buy a rug?"

"Yes, yes. She was here with a woman in a wheelchair." The woman consulted her cash register. "See here? They purchased a medium pure white ten minutes after I opened this morning."

Barely containing my excitement, I mumbled my thanks and legged it with my unwanted home accessory.

A few meters from the shop, I spied Sidney and Bernice racing down the main street. Seeing me, Sidney halted and pivoted in the opposite direction, gesturing for me to follow them back up the hill. Man and dog moved at a punishing pace, and I had to break into a sprint to catch up with them.

"What's happened?" I demanded between gasps when Sidney stopped in front of a graveyard. "Did you find the kidnappers' hideout?"

"No, but you've got to see this." He pushed open the iron gate and ushered me into the graveyard, letting go of Bernice's leash, either accidentally or by design.

The dog took off, zig-zagging between headstones until she finally stopped in front of a grave.

Throwing the blasted sheepskin rug over my shoulder, I hurried over to her.

Sidney followed at a more sedate pace and waved at the headstone, his expression triumphant. "Magdalena Moretti, beloved mother of Paolo, Patrizia, and the late Emilio."

With the exception of an extravagant (and extravagantly awful) sculpture of a cherub, the grave was unremarkable. "So what? Paolo's got to be well into his sixties. It's not surprising that his mother is pushing up daisies."

"Oh, ye of little faith." Sidney pointed over to a pair of elderly ladies seated on a bench at the far side of the graveyard. "I fell into conversation with them. They're the graveyard equivalent of bar regulars— always propping up a headstone, watching everyone come and go."

I shook my head. "I'm still not getting it. What's so special about Mama Moretti's grave?"

Sidney's gaze fell on the sheepskin rug on my shoulder, and his face contorted in horror. "And I'm not getting *that*. Please tell me you didn't buy that *thing* for our house?"

"Hardly. Now hurry and tell me about the grave."

With a shudder, he shifted his attention away from the rug and back to the headstone. "According to the ladies, Paolo and his sister only visit their mother's grave on her birthday and on high holidays. But guess who made weekly pilgrimages to this grave whenever he was in Italy?"

I gasped, realization dawning. "Not Lucky Lucchese?"

"The very man. Lucky was an assiduous visitor, always bringing fresh flowers. And unlike his brash demeanor everywhere else in Cinque Terre, he used to dress down for the occasion and sneak in, furtive-like."

"Not furtive enough, apparently," I pointed out. "Your old ladies spotted him."

"I doubt Lucky counted them as relevant. Yet they noticed him and found it odd."

"Have they mentioned this to the police?"

"Apparently not," Sidney said with a chuckle. "According to them, if the police want information, they need to ask the right questions of the right people."

My mind whirled, sifting snippets of conversation

and my mental notes on all the suspects. "The Carringtons' father was a plastic surgeon—a plastic surgeon whose practice was broken into weeks after the bank robbery."

"And Paolo Moretti's twin brother, Emilio, supposedly died in hospital after the shootout." Sidney bounced on the balls of his feet. "What if Emilio didn't die? What if he was offered immunity in exchange for information on the Amassi gang?"

"Followed by plastic surgery and a new identity?" I whistled. "It sounds like a plot from one of Lucky's books."

Sidney grinned. "Doesn't it just? Lucky was renowned for writing mobsters so convincingly. If he'd lived the life, of course, he could add authentic flavor to his characters."

Bernice began whining.

"Settle down, girl. We'll get moving again in a minute." I turned to Sidney. "Why did Lucky break into Dr. Carrington's practice? To destroy his medical records in case the Amassis went after him?"

"That's one possibility. The other is that the Amassis got wind of Emilio's treachery and sent a minion to steal his medical records and discover Emilio's new look. Either way, one thing is clear—Lucky Lucchese was probably Emilio Moretti."

Bernice began barking

A guttural squawk came from behind us. Hearts leaping, we swung around. Paolo Moretti stood staring at his mother's grave as though her ghost had come back and bitch-slapped him for being a bad boy. He held a drooping bunch of flowers in one hand.

Sidney and I had the same thought at the same time. We scanned the headstone's inscription. Today was Mama Moretti's birthday, one of the few days of the year when Paolo paid her a visit.

Babbling in Italian, Paolo backed away from the grave. Then he swung around and ran for the exit at a speed impressive for a man of his age. Before Sidney and I had time to react, Paolo leaped onto a Vespa and took off in a shower of gravel.

We looked at one another, momentarily stumped.

"So what does this mean?" I demanded. "Did Paolo kill Lucky as revenge for ratting him out all those years ago? Or did the Carrington sisters do the deed to avenge their father's murder and Heather's injury?"

Before we had the chance to debate the matter, a horn blasted. Jocelyn had pulled up in front of the graveyard in his ridiculous three-wheeled van and was gesticulating wildly. "Come on. Paolo's getting away."

We needed no more encouragement. Sidney, Bernice, and I made a beeline for the van. He and the dog leaped into the back, to be greeted by feline yowls. Not waiting to discover why the van included cats, I chucked the sheepskin rug on top of them and jumped into the passenger side.

Jocelyn hit the accelerator, and we lurched into motion, cats yowling, dog barking, Sidney howling.

As I'd noted on my drive down to Monterosso on Sunday, the mountain roads were narrow, jagged, and steep. Jocelyn rounded the curves at a terrifying speed. We'd barely covered a kilometer when he hit the brakes and we screeched to a whiplash-inducing halt.

A man stood in the middle of the road, looking like a runaway convict. His wild, shaggy red hair and bushy beard gave the impression he'd been held captive for months. His ankles were unencumbered, but he wore a pair of old-fashioned metal handcuffs around his wrists.

I opened my door and leaned out. "Del?"

My brother stared at me, slack-jawed and clueless. "Angel? What are you doing here?"

## 23

The Piaggio Ape was now packed with people, animals, and a hideous sheepskin rug. We'd squeezed Del into the vehicle by putting him in the passenger seat and me on his lap. Driving at suicidal speeds around hairpin bends with my face squashed against the windshield wasn't my idea of a fun car ride.

While Sidney failed to keep the peace between Bernice and the cats, and Jocelyn tailed Paolo's Vespa, I berated my brother. "Del, you're a complete moron. What happened? How did you escape from your kidnappers?"

"They were keeping me captive in an abandoned shack with an outhouse for a toilet. When Alessandro took me out for a pee break, I kicked him in the kidneys and left him head down in the compost loo. Then I legged it."

I glowered at him, taking in his unkempt hair and beard. "You didn't grow all that hair in just a couple of days. What are you trying to channel with your new look? Homeless stoner?"

He bristled, his defensive shields in place. "Hey, it gets cold out on fishing trips, especially at night. The beard keeps me warm."

"I've heard all about those fishing trips," I growled, working at the lock of his handcuffs with a pin. "Including your mishap with Paolo Moretti's illicit imported products. Is that why he kidnapped you? To force you to pay him back what you owed?"

Del produced his trademark wide-eyed, little boy-lost stare. It had been cute on a five-year-old boy. It was less endearing on a twenty-seven-year-old man. "Don't judge me, sis. With a baby on the way, I needed the money. It's not my fault I tripped over a rope and dropped a package into the sea."

"I doubt Paolo Moretti sees it that way. Do you know who he is? He's a convicted bank robber and probable murderer."

My brother's handcuffs opened. He shook them off and massaged his wrists. "Look, I needed a job, okay? I met Paolo's nephew Alessandro in a pub, and he said he could hook me up with work. It's difficult to find employment when you're on the run with a badly forged passport."

I exhaled hard. "You're unbelievable. Not to mention unbelievably stupid. You absconded with

Luigi Genero's wife. How do you think this story will end?"

Del was saved from answering when Jocelyn took a sharp turn into Monterosso, plunging us down a flight of steps and into the old part of town.

I'd seen Vespas and three-wheeled vans motor through the steep streets during my tour of the town, but none had moved at the speed we were traveling at now. Paolo's red Vespa zoomed down an alleyway, scattering people and animals. Jocelyn followed at a break-neck pace.

When the Vespa bumped down an even narrower series of steps, the Piaggio Ape followed. Stunned onlookers gawked at our wreck of a traveling circus. I'd become inured to the cacophony in the back, but seeing people's faces as we sped past brought Bernice and the cats back into my awareness. They'd maintained their concert all the way from Corniglia. By now, poor Sidney would have tinnitus if not total hearing loss.

That was assuming we survived the drive.

Paolo zigzagged through the market square, knocking over clothing racks and causing absolute mayhem. Not to be outdone by his rival, Jocelyn took out a jewelry stand, scattering cheap baubles all over the ground. In a bid to save himself, the jewelry seller dove headfirst into a fountain.

By this point, we'd developed a following. Small boys on scooters zoomed after us, ringing their bells.

Cyclists, young and old, followed our path of destruction. Curious pedestrians jogged to keep up.

Outside the police station, Colombo was climbing into his car, blocking the narrow street with his open door.

Jocelyn sat on his horn, leaving a gobsmacked chief inspector staring after us in horrified disbelief.

Shortly after we left Colombo in the dust, a have-a-go hero operating a road sweeper tried to create a roadblock. The dude's hair looked like it had leaped straight out of a music video for the 80s metal band Whitesnake.

The makeshift roadblock lasted all of thirty seconds.

Paolo drove straight at the road sweeper, forcing its driver into an ill-advised U-turn. The road sweeper landed on its side. The driver clambered out of the vehicle, shaking his fist and head-banging his huge hair. In a last-ditch effort to save the day, the man attempted to intercept Jocelyn's yellow three-wheeler.

Jocelyn followed Paolo's example and hit the gas. The driver saved himself from permanent damage by diving to the side, causing his fluffy wig to fly free. The man landed on his face, bald as a coot, and his huge hair landed on the road. My last sighting of the Whitesnake hair was when two of our juvenile pursuers rolled over it on their scooters, rendering it roadkill.

We were now ascending the street to Villa

Margherita. Suddenly, the import of our route hit me, and I tasted bile. Jocelyn hadn't randomly headed back to his apartment. He was following Paolo. Why was Paolo driving to the villa? Did he intend to hurt Dani?

When we reached the villa, Paolo had abandoned his Vespa outside, and the gates were open a crack. We all tumbled out of the three-wheeler—people, cats, and dog. Now that the animals were out of the back of the van, the chase was on. The cats scrambled for safety while Bernice barked and growled.

Figuring the cats could fend for themselves, I hauled a frantic Bernice into the courtyard. The door leading to the basement was wide open. Jocelyn took off like a wildcat, hurling himself down the stairs. Sidney, Del, and I followed, forcing a reluctant Bernice to accompany us.

Down in the basement, Paolo was ripping open boxes and pulling out their contents.

"What are you doing?" I demanded, bribing Bernice into silence with a dog biscuit. "What do these boxes have to do with Lucky's murder?"

"What do I care about that lying snake's death?" Paolo snarled in pure East End tones, dispensing with the pretense that he didn't speak English. "I want proof of what you said in the graveyard. Everyone knows Lucky stores his stuff in this basement while he's in the US. I need to know if that pompous, self-serving oaf truly was my brother, Emilio."

Sidney picked up the discarded photo album and

returned it to its box. "You didn't know Emilio had survived the bank robbery? You didn't kill him?"

"No, and no." Paolo threw a second photo album onto the floor in frustration. "If I'd known who Lucky really was, I'd have strangled him with my bare hands. He left me to languish in prison for fifteen years. And then he swanned back to Cinque Terre with his plastic face, flaunting his success, and laughing at all of us behind our backs. How do you think that makes me feel?"

"Not good, I imagine." I felt for the Glock in my pocket, just in case Paolo took his rage out on us. "All the same, my sympathy for you is limited. Even if you didn't murder Lucky, you kidnapped my brother and held him for ransom. And you murdered Marco."

Paolo's look could curdle milk. "You're as stupid as he is. Your brother kidnapped himself. I merely upped the stakes in his self-made adventure. And I didn't kill his pal Marco, either. My idiot nephew took him on a fishing trip, and Marco fell overboard. A tragic accident, not a murder."

Did I buy Paolo's story? The part about Marco was mighty suspicious. I'd seen the guy's caved-in skull when his body had washed up on the beach last night. His accusations about my brother, on the other hand...

I slow-blinked, a flame of anger warming me from my toes to my scalp. I pivoted on my heels and faced Del. "Is this true? Did you lure me to Monterosso under false pretenses?"

He hid behind his shaggy fringe. "Of course not. Would I do that to you?"

"In a hot second." I crossed my arms over my chest and seared him with my death ray glare. "Tell me everything. What was your master plan?"

Del suddenly found his scuffed sneakers fascinating. "We just needed a little cash to tide us over. Just enough for us to move to a new town."

"And you had the bright idea of scamming Dad and Dani's family into sending you money? Do you have any idea what you've put me through? My friend Sidney, too? We were about to fly to Florida to take a P.I. training course—a course that started yesterday. We've probably lost our places by now."

He pushed a hank of hair out of his face. "I'm sorry, Angel. Truly. I was in a desperate situation, see?"

"You're always in a desperate situation. That's your default setting. How are you going to manage a baby? You can't even cope with a dog."

"Look, I planned the kidnapping and the first ransom, but after I found the dead guy, it all went pear-shaped."

I sucked in a breath. "So you did return to the villa on Sunday morning?"

"Yeah." Del had moved from staring at his scuffed sneakers to rubbing one heel against the other. "I'd promised Marco he could borrow one of my bongs for when we were hiding out during the fake kidnap. I had to get it out of storage. Dani doesn't let me keep them in the apartment."

"My heart bleeds for you," I said sarcastically. "Hurry and get to the part where you find Lucky's body."

"No hurrying needed. I came down the stairs and tripped over the dude. He was just lying there, all bloody and gross. When I saw he was dead, I panicked. I ended up dropping a full bag of pastries on the body—my favorite, too." He looked bereft—the memory of his lost breakfast clearly still rankled. "Then I decided I'd better escape the villa in disguise in case the cops showed up."

"It didn't occur to you to call the police? You just left a naked dead man lying down here with a poker in his back?"

His head jerked up. "What poker? I didn't see any poker. And you've got the naked part wrong. Lucky was fully clothed."

Sidney and I exchanged disbelieving glances. "Are you sure?" Sidney asked. "By the time we saw Lucky's body, he was buck naked and rocking a poker in his back."

"Nah, no way. He had his clothes on. Defo." Del pointed to an area near the foot of the stairs. "The body was lying over there, on top of some kind of material that was spread over the floor."

"Lucky was naked when we saw him," I mused. "Why would the killer strip him after killing him? And where was the poker? Are you sure about what you saw?"

"Absolutely. I'm not as clever as you, Angel, but I'm not totally thick. Lucky was wearing a black suit and a white shirt and those awful shiny loafers he was always out polishing on his balcony. And there was no poker."

The details were oddly specific. Del was an inveterate liar, and a born louse, but I believed him about the body. "What happened next? How did your kidnapping master plan turn into the real deal?"

"My friends Marco and Alessandro agreed to help hide me until you delivered the ransom money. Only the moment I found the body, it all went wrong. I wasn't due to meet Alessandro until the afternoon—he was going to drive me to the hideout. But when I had to leave the villa earlier than expected, I called him for a ride."

"And he wanted to know why, and you, like the fool that you are, told him." I sighed. "For a seasoned crook, you are amazingly gullible."

"Alessandro was supposed to be my friend," Del whined. "How was I to know he'd call his uncle?"

"Because you always pick the wrong people to trust, Del. Every. Single. Time."

"Hey, I've had a terrible couple of days," Del whined. "I went from playing captive to being an actual prisoner. Look at the state of my poor wrists. I'll probably wind up with gangrene."

"Was Paolo responsible for the increase in ransom money?" Sidney asked Del, not taking his eyes off Paolo.

"Yeah. Paolo doubled the demand, not me. I knew it wouldn't wash. Dad doesn't have that kind of money, and Dani's uncle is the black sheep of their family. He's not poor, but he's not megarich like her father."

"Yeah, I get it. You're the victim." I rolled my eyes. "It's always the same story. Whatever quagmire you find yourself in is never your fault. After you wrecked my plans, I'm glad someone hogtied you in a shack."

"If you can't feel bad for me, feel bad for Marco. Poor dude wanted to let me go." Del straightened his shoulders and glared at Paolo. "That story about him falling overboard is total bull. Marco's a better sailor than Alessandro. Paolo's the one who threatened Marco when Marco wanted to go to the police. Instead of yelling at me, why don't you do your P.I. thing and arrest *him*?"

"We don't have the authority to arrest anyone," Sidney pointed out, deftly taking my arm before I pulled my Glock on Paolo.

"There's always a good old citizen's arrest," a voice said from the back of the basement.

While I'd been busy being mad at my brother and making sure Paolo didn't escape, I hadn't paid attention to what Sidney's cousin was up to. Big mistake.

Jocelyn burst out from behind a pile of boxes, wielding a spear gun. He pointed the tip at Paolo.

"Whoa, man," Del cried. "Put that down. I know a guy who lost a testicle from playing with a speargun."

"Why doesn't that surprise me?" Sidney murmured sotto voce.

Paolo put his hands up. "Put down the speargun, Jocelyn. Why would you want to hurt me?"

The reckless anger that had fueled Jocelyn's train wreck driving through town had receded, replaced by an eerie calm. "Because you're a drug smuggling, bank robbing swine who doesn't care a jot about collateral damage. My father died in the shootout after you and your lowlife friends robbed that bank."

Paolo bowed his head, giving a convincing act of contrition. "I'm sorry that happened. It was a long time ago, and I was a different person than the man I am today."

"The man you are today supplies drugs to teenagers," Jocelyn shot back, speargun still trained on the older man. "Am I supposed to believe that's an improvement?"

I never got to hear whatever lie Paolo had been about to tell. A commotion in the courtyard drew my attention away from the speargun shenanigans. A moment later, the door burst open, and several armed police officers swarmed down the stairs and into the basement, neatly surrounding us.

"Put the speargun down, Mr. Dingus-Cockett," Chief Inspector Colombo said, descending the stairs at a more leisurely pace than his comrades. "And come out from behind those boxes, Moretti, hands on your head. Now, which of you fools is going to tell me what possessed you to tear through town like bats on mopeds?"

Jocelyn placed the speargun on the ground. "I'll surrender my weapon, but in return, I expect you to do your job. That man—" he jabbed a finger in Paolo's direction, "—imports drugs from Marseilles. And I have reason to believe that he murdered a young man named Marco La Malfa."

"All lies," Paolo cried. "This man writes books about aliens. He's crazy."

The situation devolved into a farce when Del added his incoherent two cents to the story, babbling about lost pastries and sore wrists.

Colombo held up a hand and turned his granite gaze on me. "Why don't you tell me what's going on?"

Keeping my account concise, I summed up the events of the past couple of days, detailing everything from Del's first text message to our theory that Lucky Lucchese was Emilio Moretti.

The chief inspector didn't blink the entire time I spoke, which I found unnerving. When I'd finished, he gave a curt nod. "That ties in with what we know. Emilio Moretti received immunity in return for information on the Amassi gang. Part of the deal was extensive facial reconstruction and a new identity."

"What about my brother's claim that he found

Lucky's body in the basement, fully clothed and poker-free?"

"We found fibers consistent with the outfit he described in the wound. Also pastry crumbs. We assume Lucky was stripped after death, and the lethal weapon placed back into the wound to add to the dramatic effect when his body was discovered in Mr. Dingus-Cockett's apartment."

"So Lucky *was* killed in the basement?" Sidney asked. "Not in Jocelyn's apartment?"

Colombo's shrug was intriguingly noncommittal. "Maybe. We're still looking for the stolen tent that was placed on the floor under the body. Also, we've found no sign of Lucky's clothes or wallet."

"What about Moretti?" Jocelyn demanded. "Aren't you going to arrest him?"

"For his crazy driving, certainly. For the other alleged crimes, let's just say you haven't told me anything I didn't already know." Colombo's lips drew back in a scary smile. "You'll also have some questions to ask about *your* driving. You nearly lobbed off my side mirror."

An ambulance siren wailed, coming closer by the second. Colombo frowned and checked his radio. "Don't tell me something else has happened at this house of horrors?"

A young officer appeared at the top of the stairs. "Sir, an ambulance has just pulled in. The woman in apartment six is giving birth."

## 24

*S*houting orders for Paolo and Jocelyn to be brought to the station for questioning, Colombo raced up the basement stairs. Del and I followed suit, leaving Bernice in Sidney's care.

When we charged into Del and Dani's apartment, Dani was in the bedroom, half-naked and coated in sweat. It'd been a while since I'd attended a biology class, but even I recognized how far along this labor was. That ambulance would have to wait until it had two patients to transport.

Lucy Carrington stood at the business end of the bed, her medical supplies laid out neatly on a tray. "One more push, Dani. The head's almost out. On the next contraction, give me all you've got."

Dani reared up with a huff, a puff, and a roar and pushed until she turned tomato red. I experienced a cramp of sympathy, although I was happy to admit I had no idea what she was going through. Del lurched to her side and held her hand just as their baby girl made her earthside debut.

Colombo made a discreet retreat into the living room, but I was too stunned to look away.

"There we go," Lucy said, wrapping the baby in a towel and placing her on Dani's chest. "You have a beautiful daughter."

Dani and Del stared at their baby, utterly enraptured. All I saw was a squirming, red-faced, red-haired alien being.

"She's perfect," Dani said between sobs.

Del, who'd always been one of life's great criers, was a blubbering mess. "She's the most beautiful thing I've ever made."

I blinked to get rid of a curious stinging sensation. Dust must have gotten in my eyes. I wasn't crying—absolutely not. I took a step back from the bed. I needed to distance myself from this hormonal, emotional maelstrom.

Colombo reappeared at the bedroom door and laid a hand on my shoulder. "We should give the new parents some time alone."

I needed no further encouragement. Leaving Lucy to cope with the delivery of the afterbirth, Colombo and I drank coffee in the living room, and I filled him in on the rest of the story.

"I'm sorry I didn't tell you the whole truth when you questioned me, but I was working under the assumption that my brother had been kidnapped. Also, I didn't know if I could trust you. I wondered if you were on the make, especially when I saw you shaking hands with Paolo Moretti on the beach last night."

"Ah, the old story about my house not matching my salary." Colombo didn't appear in the least offended. "That house has been in my family for three generations. As for my relationship with Paolo Moretti, what's that saying? Keep your friends close and your enemies closer?"

There was a knock at the apartment door, and Sidney popped his head in. "I want to get food for Bernice, and I really need to get this rug away from her. She growls at it like it's a wild animal stealing her food stash."

"Tie her up outside and give her food and water. Then come in here and talk to us." I took the sheepskin rug and showed it to Chief Inspector Colombo.

I'd just finished telling him about my rug theory in a hushed voice when Sidney joined us in the living room. "Angel's idea isn't too much of a stretch," he remarked, also keeping the volume low. "Especially as we have proof that Lucy Carrington purchased a rug just like the one placed under the body."

"Why buy another rug?" Colombo looked from me to Sidney. "Why bother?"

"Because the Carringtons are staying in a temporary rental apartment," I explained. "As soon as the cleaner came after they checked out, the rug would be missed."

The bedroom opened, ending our conversation. Lucy Carrington emerged, shutting the door behind her. She looked tired, but content.

Colombo gestured to an empty armchair. "Please sit, Dr. Carrington. I think you might be able to help with my investigation."

Lucy's serene expression was gone in a flash. She gulped, her composure slipping. "I don't know what more I can say. I've told you everything I know."

"Not quite everything," I said, holding her gaze. "We know your father performed plastic surgery on Lucky Lucchese thirty-five years ago. And we're also aware that your father was killed when a burglar broke into his practice. That same attack left your sister in a wheelchair."

Lucy's entire body crumpled, and large, fat tears flowed down her moon face. She collapsed in an armchair and buried her face in her hands. "It's all been such a nightmare."

"Why don't you tell us what happened?" Colombo posed the question in a gentler, less confrontational manner than I'd grown to expect from the man.

The doctor took a moment to pull herself together. "Lucky, Emilio—whatever he called himself—destroyed my family. My father gave him a new face. There was no need for Lucky to come back to look for his medical records. My father intended to destroy them as soon as he received the go-ahead from the appropriate department. Instead, Lucky got impatient, and chose the one evening to break in that my father was at the practice with Heather."

"I'm so sorry, Lucy," I said gently. "That must have been awful for you, and especially for Heather. How did you discover that Lucky Lucchese was the man who killed your father?"

"When our mother died two years ago, Heather and I inherited all of her papers. Among the boxes, we discovered Emilio Moretti's medical files. After all that fuss, it turned out my father hadn't kept Emilio's records at the practice, but at home in his safe." Lucy twisted the rings on her chubby fingers. "Seeing Emilio's new face brought back all the old hatred."

Sidney leaned forward in his chair with a puppy dog eagerness that made me smile. "How did you figure out Emilio was Lucky Lucchese? After over thirty years, surely he'd be hard to recognize from the after photos your father took following his operations?"

"I became obsessed with finding him," Lucy said, becoming more sure of herself as the tale tumbled out. "I hired an expert in facial analysis to provide me with a mockup of what he'd look like today. Even when I received the picture, I figured finding the man would be a needle-in-haystack situation. So you can imagine my surprise when I saw that same face on the back of a book I'd borrowed from the library."

"Once you knew Emilio was Lucky Lucchese," I

said, "all you had to do was read one of the many interviews he's given over the years to discover Lucky spends half the year in Monterosso. So you hatched a plan to stay at the same villa where Lucky has his apartment."

Colombo, who'd sat slumped in an armchair, content to let Sidney and I ask questions, now adopted that predatory look I remembered all too well from my sojourn at the Monterosso police station. "If you've done your research on Lucky Lucchese, you'll know he only lives in Monterosso during the summer. Why choose November to visit?"

"I only discovered Lucky's identity a month ago," Lucy replied in clipped tones. "Heather's not well, and she'll be too ill to travel in the summer—if she makes it that far. This was our only chance to confront Emilio together. I wanted to give her closure before she died."

"So you lured Lucky to Monterosso on a pretext. And then what? You attacked him?"

"What?" The woman's eyes widened, and she shook her head vehemently. "No, you don't understand. I told Lucky we had some important information to share with him about the money stolen during the bank robbery. Lucky got none of the money, remember? He traded that chance for a new face and fast freedom."

"As Lucky Lucchese, Emilio had a successful career," Sidney interjected. "Why would he risk all that for money stolen decades ago?"

ZARA KEANE

"Greed," I said. "Think of all the product placement-style deals Lucky made with local businesses. Think of his decision to rent an apartment rather than buy a house. Lucky enjoyed having money —the more, the better."

Colombo shifted impatiently in his seat. "Moving back to your meeting with Lucky Lucchese—you persuaded him to meet you in Monterosso. What happened when you finally came face to face with the man who murdered your father and injured your sister? Did you see red and grab a poker?"

Lucy's mouth moved, but nothing came out.

"No, that's not what happened."

We swung around to see Heather in the open doorway. A shocked Barbie and Ken stood behind her wheelchair, clearly agog at what they'd overheard.

Heather pushed her chair forward, coming to rest at the foot of the steps. She stared up at him, chin held high, eyes defiant. "If you don't want to be overheard, do a better job at closing doors. You left the door open a crack."

Sidney reddened. "That was my fault. I had trouble getting it to close after I gave Bernice her food and water."

Colombo got to his feet and lumbered down the steps from the living room to the small entrance hall, coming to stand next to Heather's wheelchair. "What can you add to your sister's account of your meeting with Lucky Lucchese?"

Heather slid her sister a glance before responding. "There was no meeting. We planned to speak to him and tell him who we were. I wanted to look him in the eye and see him recognize me, acknowledge how his actions cost us our father and me a normal life."

"So what happened when Lucky showed up at your apartment?" I demanded. "Lucky didn't stick a poker in his own back."

"I don't know what happened," Heather replied, her cool eyes snapping at me. "When Lucy and I entered our apartment on Sunday afternoon, Lucky was lying dead in front of the fireplace, naked with a poker in his back."

I gasped. "Wait—you're saying you didn't kill Lucky?"

Heather treated me to a poisonous once-over. "Of course we didn't kill him. We wanted closure, not a dead body. I wanted to see the man who killed my father and left me for dead. No more, no less. I figured I deserved at least that from him."

"But you didn't get your chance," Colombo finished, "because he was already dead by the time you and your sister reached Monterosso, just as you claimed in your statements."

"Exactly." Lucy came down the steps and took her sister's hand. "We didn't kill Lucky, but I'm responsible for moving his body upstairs to Jocelyn's apartment. Heather allowed me to use her wheelchair, and I transported him in the lift."

Barbie gave a strangled cry. "Why? What had Jocelyn done to you?"

"Nothing, but I knew Lucky lived at apartment one when he was at the villa. What better place for him to be found dead?"

"And the white sheepskin rug," I said, holding up the remnants of the smaller version I'd purchased that morning. "Why did you place the body on the rug?"

"It didn't seem right to leave him lying on the tiles," Heather whispered. "Not even he deserved that. I suggested using the rug. It only occurred to me later that the absence of the rug when we checked out would put us under suspicion of his murder."

"Why did you leave the poker in the body?" The chief inspector asked, now appearing more intrigued than interrogatory. "Surely it was difficult to move the body with the poker still in his back."

"Of course I removed it," Lucy said, giving him a withering look. "I left that poker in our apartment and used one of Jocelyn's when I laid out the body. All the apartments on that side of the building have the same style of fireplace and pokers."

The chief inspector's expression gave little away. "That's a pleasant story, ladies, but it leaves us with something of a conundrum. If you didn't murder Lucky, then who did?"

## 25

*I* scanned our gallery of suspects: Lucy, Heather, Ken, and Barbie. All wore guilty expressions. All looked as though they'd rather be anywhere else than crammed into Del and Dani's cramped entrance hall.

My gaze came to rest on Barbie. "I think I know who killed Lucky, Chief Inspector. And I think I know why."

Feeling the weight of my stare, Barbie flinched and took a step back. "Why are you staring at me like that? I know nothing about Lucky's death. How many times do I have to say it?"

With silent stealth, Sidney moved behind our suspects and blocked the exit, leaving me to do the talking. "You and Ken live in apartment three. According to Lucy, all the apartments on the left side of the villa have identical open fireplaces, complete with identical fire pokers. That means your apartment has the same setup as Jocelyn's and the Carrington's apartment."

"So what?" Barbie's voice was shrill, her eyes panic-stricken. "I had no reason to want Lucky dead."

"But that's not quite true, is it?" I was aware I was swimming into the realm of guesswork, but I was confident I'd stay afloat. "Two years ago, you were living in L.A., trying to break into the American TV and movie market. At that time, Lucky was also in L.A., negotiating his Crimeflix deal. You auditioned for one of his TV shows."

Her breath came in quick gasps. "So what if I did? I auditioned for a lot of shows."

"What happened?" I asked, more gently this time. "Did Lucky promise you a role in return for sexual favors?"

Her hand flew to her mouth, but she didn't speak.

"And when you discovered he'd used you and had no intention of giving you a role in one of his book adaptations, you were devastated."

"You have no idea what that world is like." She was crying now, the fight gone out of her. "Casting call after casting call, sleazy actors, directors, producers, and agents. Everyone promises you the world, but no one means what they say. After eighteen months of rejections, I couldn't take it anymore. I vowed the audition for the lead role in the TV adaptation of Lucky's novel, *Final Target*, would be my last. Hooking up with Lucky was supposed to seal the deal. Instead, I didn't even get a callback. And you know the worst part? When I moved into the villa and bumped into him in the courtyard, *he didn't even recognize me.*"

"Barbie, say nothing else without a lawyer." Ken stepped forward and put a hand on her shoulder. "I mean it, babe. Not one word."

She shoved off his hand and rounded on him. "Don't you start. You're no better than the Luckys of this world. You promised me a new life in Italy, not a dead-end job slinging gelato."

"It's only temporary." Smug Ken didn't look too sure of himself now. "Just until I get my new company off the ground."

"Ken," she shouted, "that will never happen. Word gets around. No one wants to invest in anything you're involved with. You're financial kryptonite."

"What happened between you and Lucky?" Chief Inspector Colombo steered the conversation away from Barbie's woes and back to the murder. "Why did you kill him?"

Her caterpillar eyelashes fluttered, smudging her cheeks with dry mascara flakes. "I didn't mean to hurt him, I swear."

She darted a glance at the door, but Sidney blocked her path.

"Tell me what happened," Colombo repeated. "One piece at a time."

She exhaled like a deflating balloon. Ken took her

by the arms and supported her. "Say the word, and I'll get you a lawyer."

"It doesn't matter, Ken. Nothing matters anymore. It's over, don't you see? Whatever I say or don't say, they'll find out what I did." Taking a deep breath, she squared her shoulders and faced the crowd. "On Saturday night, I was home alone. Ken was at a conference in Milan, and he crashed at a coworker's place. I fixed dinner and settled down to binge-watch TV. Around two o'clock in the morning, I heard noises in apartment five, the one below ours. I was concerned because no one was supposed to be staying there until next week. Our landlord informs us of new arrivals ahead of time, so we know to expect them."

"We made a last-minute booking," Heather interjected. "Perhaps your landlord forgot to mention it."

"Yes, but we didn't arrive until Sunday afternoon," Lucy pointed out. "I assume the person Barbie heard in the apartment was Lucky."

With a curt nod, Barbie resumed her story. "Anyway, I was worried, so I knocked on a few doors to see if anyone would come downstairs with me. Everyone was out, or not answering. I debated what to do, and I finally went down and see for myself."

I raised an eyebrow. "Grabbing a handy-dandy poker on your way out the door?"

She flushed. "As a matter of fact, yes. When I knocked on the door to apartment five, I was amazed when Lucky opened it. He was drunk and obnoxious. Lucky was often drunk and obnoxious, and I'd learned to avoid him when he was intoxicated. This time, he was a messy drunk."

"Did you think about calling the police?" Sidney asked. "If you were scared?"

"He asked me in for a drink," Barbie said, ignoring Sidney's question. "When I refused, he turned up the volume on his music system. I got annoyed and told him to keep the noise down. He just laughed at me and said he'd recognized me all along. He just didn't want me to get clingy. Then he had the nerve to ask if I wanted a repeat performance of our night together in L.A."

"What happened next?" Colombo pressed when she trailed off. "How did Lucky die?"

Barbie took a deep breath before answering. "Lucky saw how I reacted when he mentioned us having sex. He found it hilarious. He scooped a sheaf of papers off the coffee table and dangled it in front of me. It was a pilot script for yet another of his stupid TV adaptations. I refused to take it, so he went back to his pile of scripts to find another morsel to taunt me with. At that moment, I saw red. I don't remember stabbing him. One second, the poker was in my hand. The next, it was in Lucky's back." Her voice broke on a sob. "It all happened so fast. One second, I was a regular person. The next, I was a murderer."

Ken slipped his hand around Barbie's. "I can pick

up the story from here. After Barbie realized what she'd done, she called me. I drove back from Milan straight away, and we hatched a plan. We planned to dump Lucky at sea. I knew Saul and Riccardo kept a tent in the basement, and I suggested wrapping the body in the tent before transporting it in our car. It was still dark when we carried the body down to the basement. We didn't dare use the lift in case anyone remembered hearing it in use. We'd just laid the body on the tent when we heard footsteps."

"That was my brother," I said dryly, "in search of his bong collection. Imagine his surprise at what he found instead."

"We crouched behind a stack of boxes waiting for him to leave." Barbie wrinkled her nose. "He took his sweet time about it. I still don't get why he needed to put on a dreadlocks wig and a fake beard."

"Very few of my brother's decisions make logical sense," I said, "but go on with your story. Why didn't you dump Lucky's body at sea as you'd planned?"

Ken picked up the story. "Once we knew Jimmy had seen the body, we were afraid he'd call the police. I knew there'd be fibers and maybe DNA from Barbie and me on the body. And after he spilled a bag of pastries, there were crumbs everywhere."

"So we took him back to apartment five," Barbie said. "We stripped him, washed him, and dumped him in front of the fireplace, replacing the poker in his back. Then we cleaned up as best we could."

"We put the bloodstained tent and Lucky's clothes into the boot of my car," Ken added, "and I drove them to a dump just outside Genoa. I cleaned the boot as best I could, but I was worried about leftover evidence."

"You took the car to be cleaned, right?" I suggested, the puzzle pieces arranging themselves neatly.

"Yes," Ken admitted, "but not until Monday. I cleaned the boot several times, but I couldn't shift the feeling I'd missed something. I drove to a garage in Levanto and checked in my car for a deep clean."

"That's why you took the train back to Monterosso on Monday evening," Sidney said, a look of triumph on his face. "Hence you meeting Maria Bianchi on the train and offering to walk her back to the villa once Barbie finished work."

"Telling the story now makes it sound like we were organized." Barbie's laughter was laced with bitterness. "We weren't. If we'd had a proper plan, maybe we'd have pulled it off. But how were we to know the Carringtons would arrive a few hours after we returned Lucky's body to apartment five?"

"Right," Ken continued. "We assumed Lucky was renting the place on his own. We thought leaving the body there would buy us time until either Jimmy showed up with the police, or we got the chance to take the body out on the boat as originally planned."

"I'm truly sorry," Barbie sobbed. "I never meant to

hurt him. It all happened so fast. I'm not a killer, I swear. It was just a moment of madness."

Chief Inspector Colombo spoke into his radio. A moment later, a procession of police officers trooped into Del and Dani's apartment to read people their rights and escort them to Monterosso's tiny police station. Barbie was arrested for Lucky's murder, and Ken for helping her after the fact. The Carrington sisters would have to answer to charges of tampering with evidence and failing to report a crime.

The vroom of engines in the courtyard preceded the sound of wheels churning gravel. Soon, the only people left outside apartment six were Colombo, Sidney, and me.

Bernice, who'd taken the unfolding drama in her stride, was happily chewing on a bone she'd unearthed from a flowerpot.

Colombo slid my ID card out of his breast pocket and presented it to me with a bow. "You're free to go, Ms. Doyle." A hint of humor threatened to erode his resting grumpy face. "With a full legal blessing—I'm aware you have an Irish passport squirreled away somewhere."

I schooled my features into an expression of extreme innocence. "Did I not mention I'm a dual national?"

"No, you left that part out, alongside your association with the Omega Group." He dipped his head. "I've met your mother. Desirée Chablis is a remarkable woman."

"You couldn't put in a good word for us, could you?" Sidney smiled sweetly. "Only we're not at the top of her list of favorite people right now."

This triggered a genuine, hearty laugh. "I'll bear that in mind, Mr. Foggington-Smythe. By the way, your cousin won't be behind bars for long. He'll lose his driving license for a while, but I don't see any reason to charge him for holding a speargun." His radio crackled into life, producing a grimace. "I need to deal with my motley collection of villains. No offence, but I hope we won't meet again during your stay in Monterosso. Have a safe trip home."

After Chief Inspector Colombo left, Sidney leaned down and whispered, "Are you still carrying that Glock?"

"Yep." I grinned. "You?"

He winked at me. "Guilty as *not* charged."

I tugged his arm and pulled him toward Dani's room. "Come and meet my niece. She looks like an alien spawn, but she's kind of adorable." I knocked on the door. "Are you three decent? I want to show off my niece to my friend, Sidney."

There was no response. I looked up at Sidney and pulled a face. "I hope they're not doing anything they shouldn't. The doctor said no shenanigans until at least six weeks postpartum."

I knocked again, and a sliver of angst pierced my

moment of harmony. Opening the door a crack at a time, I eased into Del and Dani's bedroom, feeling the breeze from the wide-open window.

The room was empty. No brother, no new mother, and definitely no baby.

I swore aloud in several languages. "That low-down louse. That sneaky serpent. That egregious piece of excrement."

"Are you done abusing alliteration and slaughtering the English language?"

"No." I added a few choice phrases that would make a sailor blush.

Sidney scooped a piece of paper off the unmade bed and handed it to me.

*Hey, Sis. Thanks for your help, even if you didn't score us the money. Dani's nervous Paolo Moretti has figured out who she is. We're heading south for a while. I'll be in touch when the coast is clear.*

*Del xx*

*P.S. Dani says Bernice really likes you and we want you to have her as a thank-you gift. Her papers are in the drawer under the stove. She's got one of those chip things.*

*P.P.S. The baby's name is Desdemona Jade.*

"The rat. He planned to land me with that blasted dog before he hit send on the first text message." I stomped through the apartment and threw open the door. "With all the commotion in the courtyard, I didn't hear them drive away. Looks like they stole Jocelyn's yellow Piaggio Ape."

"Not a bad choice," Sidney mused. "It's not like Jocelyn will drive anything for the foreseeable."

Bernice abandoned her bone and greeted us with an excited yelp. I stroked her soft fur.

"Del has your number," Sidney said, laughing. "You're totally taking that dog home with you."

"Question is, where is home?" I mused, staring out at the shimmering sea. "And what are we going to do about our boot camp? I don't know how easy it is to bring a dog to the US, chip or no chip."

Sidney put his arm around my shoulders. It felt nice—secure, dependable, and surprisingly warm. "Let's tackle one problem at a time."

Bernice wagged her tail and performed the little jig I was learning to recognize. I slid Sidney a wicked grin. "Okay, Mr. Cool and Collected. Here's the first problem for you to tackle: we're fresh out of poop bags."

∾

 Thanks so much for reading *Murdered in Monterosso*. I hope you enjoyed Angel and Sidney's third international adventure! If you'd like to see photos and info on their

travel itinerary in the book, plus read an exclusive bonus scene, sign up for the bonus PDF at

**zarakeane.com/murdered-in-monterosso-bonus**

Happy Reading!
*Zara x*

**Join my mailing list and get news, giveaways, and free stories!**

**Sign up on zarakeane.com/travelpinewsletter**

ALSO BY ZARA KEANE

## TRAVEL P.I.

## MOVIE CLUB MYSTERIES

## TIME-SLIP MYSTERIES

# ABOUT THE AUTHOR

*USA Today* bestselling author Zara Keane grew up in Dublin, Ireland, but spent her summers in a small town very similar to the fictitious Whisper Island in the Movie Club Mysteries.

She currently lives in Switzerland with her family. When she's not writing, Zara loves knitting, running, unplugged gaming, and adding to her insanely large lipstick collection.

Zara has an active Facebook reader group, **Zara Keane's Mystery Mavens**, where she chats, shares snippets of upcoming stories, and hosts members-only giveaways. She hopes to join you for a virtual coffee very soon!

zarakeane.com